NICK OF TIME

Other Books by Sallie Bingham

Cory's Feast (Novel), Sunstone Press

The Hub of the Miracle (Poems), Sunstone Press

After Such Knowledge (Novel), Houghton-Mifflin

The Touching Hand (Novella and Short Stories), Houghton-Mifflin

> "There is no doubt about it—Sallie Bingham can hold her own with many of the best stylists writing in America today." *The Chicago Tribune*

The Way It Is Now (Short Stories), Viking Press

> "The people of whom Bingham writes in these 15 stories come alive through her penetrating characterizations." *Booklist*

Passion and Prejudice, A Family Memoir, Alfred A. Knopf

> "Sallie Bingham's lively account of her life has the feel of a novel." *The New Yorker*

> "A feisty figure with an eye for hypocrisy, Bingham creates images of the world of the Binghams with a kind of iron grace." *The New York Times Book Review*

Upstate (Novel), Permanent Press

Small Victories (Novel), Zoland Books

> "An absorbing novel." *The New York Times Book Review*

Matron of Honor (Novel), Zoland Books

> "This powerful narrative is her best yet." *Publishers Weekly*

Straight Man (Novel), Zoland Books

Transgressions (Short Stories), Sarabande Press

> "These are marvelous stories of experience and have the ripeness of wry, hard-won wisdom." *Phillip Lopate*

NICK OF TIME

A Novel by
Sallie Bingham

SUNSTONE
PRESS
SANTA FE

The events, people, and incidents in this story are the sole product of the
author's imagination. The story is fictional and any resemblance
to individuals living or dead is purely coincidental.

—

Book and cover design by Vicki Ahl

Sunstone books may be purchased for educational, business, or sales promotional use.
For information please write: Special Markets Department, Sunstone Press,
P.O. Box 2321, Santa Fe, New Mexico 87504-2321.

Library of Congress Cataloging-in-Publication Data:

Bingham, Sallie.
  Nick of time / by Sallie Bingham.
     p. cm.
  Includes bibliographical references and index.
  ISBN 0-86534-523-6 (alk. paper) --   ISBN 0-86534-524-4 (pbk. : alk. paper)
  1. Ballroom dancing--Fiction. 2. Middle-aged women--Fiction.
  3. Self-realization--Fiction. I. Title.

PS3552.I5C67 2005
813'.54--dc22

                                        2006019873

WWW.SUNSTONEPRESS.COM
SUNSTONE PRESS / POST OFFICE BOX 2321 / SANTA FE, NM 87504-2321 /USA
(505) 988-4418 / ORDERS ONLY (800) 243-5644 / FAX (505) 988-1025

Change the rhythm, and the walls of the city will shake.

—Pindar

1

I'll die happy, knowing I'm the best social dancer in Santa Fe.

They used to recognize me in all the clubs: dark spangled Alegria out on Aqua Fria where the population's mixed on Friday nights—a lot of local people, some of them fine dancers—and wild on Saturdays with the illegals streaming in from a week of hauling and digging; spacey echoing Rodeo Nites—David, the bartender, is a friend of mine—where the older crowd from the motels goes to practice their routines; and the best place of all as far as I'm concerned, the open roof of the old La Fonda Hotel on Sunday evenings in summer, when the Country-Western band from Taos gets started, and the double domes of the cathedral across the street glow with their own yellow light, and the stars look very clear and very far away, as though they're shining for all of us:

the grandmas in their tiered skirts, twirling their hearts out as their for-this-one-night-only cowboy husbands reel them in like kites catching a stiff breeze;

the younger women, alone and watching, arms crossed, on the sidelines—they come in twos and threes—not above tapping a neat custom boot with regulation incising and silver-medallion-decorated instep strap to tunes they want to be moving to—and will be soon, swept up by someone like me;

the young couples, nurses, accountants, who knows; they're dressed up for the occasion in short skirts and new-looking cowboy hats, trying out the steps they learned at the dance studio during the past week;

and me in my black dress clothes, my "costume" some wise-ass called it, working my way around the floor, stepping and twirling and rolling them out, never long with one partner—and there's hardly a woman I've met, on the roof of La Fonda in the gleaming summer night, who didn't leave me happier with herself than she was when she first came into my arms.

That was my goal, to the extent that I had one:

To dance some soul into those women, and into me, for that matter. Life's had a drying effect on me—whose life hasn't?—and now I'm fifty-five I know there's not much time left to get back into the dew.

There's several ways of doing that: all night drinking parties with good friends (and calling in sick next day), making my old bed in the Wilderness Buck and I share shake the wall (and waking up saddle-sore), buying myself a dozen red roses I can't afford (and hearing Buck grouse when the credit card bill comes in). I've done them all and more, but none of them are as sweet and juicy as the feel of a full skirt against my knees and the floor satin-smooth under my boot soles and one of those old C&W tunes flowing down my legs like liquid silver. That's dancing.

Warm summer nights, not much air stirring, and when I was taking a break, catching my breath as I leaned against the railing that kept us all from falling straight down onto Cathedral Place, the smell—sweet, salty—and the look—bright, moving—came at me all at once, and I knew this was what I was put on the earth to do.

During the week, I live the life they could have predicted for me when my parents carried me up to the baptismal font at the little church in the Purchase, where my aunt and uncle promised guidance in the way of the Lord (he gave me a silver Mint Julep cup, she just left me alone). But the way I turned out is not what they imagined or expected:

My look: black jeans, washed, pressed, starched; black ruffle-front shirt and leather vest; black Stetson and cowhide boots with medium heel I bought with my whole paycheck, three years ago.

Boots are a good investment. Most things I've wanted are worth just about exactly what I paid for them, but my boots have doubled and tripled their original value; resoled and re-heeled from time to time, they'll last me out, and if I have my wishes, I'll be wearing them when I meet my maker.

I started writing this on the feast day of St. John the Baptist, who knew something about the value of footwear. I was sitting at the kitchen table in this mobile home called Wilderness, about ten miles south of Santa Fe. There was no particular reason to start then rather than when I'm on my deathbed, telling as much as I can remember into a tape-recorder for my granddaughter, little Melly (named for me). I hadn't been diagnosed with cancer; I was still fibrous and sturdy as the big Ponderosa Pine outside this window, that's straight as a ruler and smells of vanilla and orange. I was just back from my first trip as the-person-I-thought-I-was to New York (there was another trip, a long time ago, with my parents), and I was relishing at least some aspects of it.

I went to New York because people there wanted to hear my story—my special take on dancing.

You see, I like to lead. In fact leading's at the core of it—what drew me to dancing in the first place. No, I'm not gay, wouldn't dream of it. I like a man between my legs. But there's a giving of pleasure I never found, even there, a sureness and lightness bright as a summer day. You should see those smiles, the ones I drew when I put my arm around them and started them moving. Old, young, fat, thin—it didn't matter. Maybe life had dried them out, too, and this was the one drop of sweetness: to be moved, to fold into the curve of another person's body. Male, female, does it matter? A baby who doesn't know any better will fit into any shoulder or arm. So why not us? Why not take the pleasure of moving together, no matter who the other one is? Sometimes we sing, the words and the music melting along one curve. "Souls cleave," my mother, bless her, used to say. Strip away all the other stuff, and that's what you see: souls cleaving, to the beat. That's what I offered, and I'll be eternally glad I did.

It happened at La Fonda. The dancing there on a Sunday night was the honey that drew them.

CBS was working on a magazine piece about Santa Fe and decided to include a segment on Country-Western dancers. I was there dancing the evening they taped.

My way of moving hit those people like a revelation: how you can stand anything during the week (and most people have to stand a good deal) if you can step out on the weekend and put your arms around someone and get her started.

The hotel management was all for the taping—tourism's down in Santa Fe because of recent events on the other side of the country. So everyone was pleased as punch when the cameras arrived one blue evening with the spooled and unspooled and unspooling cables and the dollies loaded with equipment and the tall glaring lights.

Those praying mantis lights took over half the dance floor, and the cables were snaking everywhere, a threat to high-steppers. But we managed to cram ourselves into the space they left us, and we put on a pretty good show. Most of the regulars were there, dressed up and juiced by the excitement: "We're going to be on national TV!" A couple of kids were running around asking people their names, deciding who to interview, asking us to sign releases.

One of them came up to me when I was dancing with Gayway

Kinsel: a made-up name like a lot of them here, replacing something more ordinary, like Mary Ann Smith—a whole history, probably, left behind someplace like Minneapolis.

At first I thought the CBS kid was going to leave me alone and stick to Gayway; she was pretty as a picture that night in her white lace skirt, swaying out over a fine pair of legs, and she has a story that holds almost anyone's attention.

It was too ordinary for the kid, I guess: messed-up love, brawling, a pickup packed with contraband heading for a new life in the West.

So the kid turned to me.

I saw him look at me once, do the usual double-take, then glance down at his clipboard as though he hoped he'd find a category there for me.

"Name?" he asked, still hoping for the expected, some Tom or Wayne or Harry with just enough Western flavor to give it that true smoky tang.

When I told him my name, he heard my voice and knew there was no category for me on his sheet.

He peered up at me—I'm five eleven in my boots—like he still hoped against hope for a glimpse of some stubble.

"You're . . ." he said finally, and couldn't go any further.

Then he—this nameless kid—made a decision that changed my life.

He went for the head honcho.

A week later, I was driving south to the airport in Albuquerque for my first trip to New York as a dancer.

It wouldn't be the St. Regis in those glow years just after the war, the way it was that other visit: patent-leather shoes with a strap across the instep, charcoal-gray suit and straw hat with a black-velvet streamer—the right kind of visitor for the right kind of city, the one my mother concocted for me to match her somewhat-privileged youth.

Not that the glamour held for me, even then: I did something I can't remember in the hotel dining room, something having to do with a lobster, my first encounter, and was sent up to my room in disgrace, patent-leather shoes and all; and lay on a pea-green silk love seat and wept big, staining tears for the life I'd left behind in Kentucky.

The memory of that misery made me doubt entering the lists again, even flying—as I thought—my true colors. I made a last-ditch attempt at undoing the whole sequence, the way when I was growing up I'd jerk the grimy stitches out of a sampler. I called the producer and told him I was nothing special, really; Santa Fe was full of freaks more interesting than me, like the guy in hiking boots and a pastel dress you could find any day composing his memoirs in the library.

This producer was a smart guy. He said something that went right to me: "We've got plenty of interesting types for this show already lined up, but you have a message that's going to mean something to a lot of women."

Not just a meaningless little life with its evaporating satisfactions but something like the trumpet of Jericho, sounding before the tumbling walls—that's what he heard. You can't do anything but follow that trumpet, whip lashed around from time to time but mostly riding the craving like a wild horse only partly manageable even with strong thighs and knees.

It was fifty years, half a century, since my visit to the St. Regis and its lobster, and I was riding down to Albuquerque in my pickup, Bonnie Raitt turned up high, and the world my oyster, as my father, God bless his heart, said when he looked me over in my first prom dress.

La Bajada did give me a warning.

It's the first steep hill you hit, driving south out of Santa Fe. The Spanish conquistadors topped that hill sometime in the sixteenth century and looked down for the first time on my dusty little town. I was trapped in the slow lane behind a semi hitting its Jake brakes, and while I waited to pass, I had one of those glimpses I don't want to call a vision:

a little Indian boy at the end of a procession.

Maybe a priest's helper, or a conquistador's slave, or maybe just a tag-along, trying to survive, even having the gall to want to thrive;

rags, and bare feet, and hungry, and not much interested in the low mud houses down in the valley unless they meant a crust gnawed in an alley.

I didn't pay any attention. I wanted, I wanted badly, to be seen and heard—to be a light unto the nations, and a glory to the people of Israel.

A prophet, you ask?

Is she crazy?

A priestess, of what?

All I can tell you is I hungered to blow my trumpet on national television, to see some walls somewhere quake, even if I didn't have enough strength to bring them tumbling down.

That little Indian boy was a warning, although I didn't know it, then.

Feed my sheep, the Man said, and here I was leaving everything that had fed me, and fully, in order to be seen, to be heard.

What does that cost?

I never wondered. I was full of Bonnie and my own importance, because some people from what we all know is the capital of the universe had recognized me for who I am.

You know how Bonnie sings, "Heart of a Stranger," and your good feelings start to stream like water toward all those women she sings to, all those women still hoping and waiting? How can anyone spare herself good feelings—fellow feelings—for those who still wait and hope?

Love.

What we want.

Only who, these days, has the nerve to ask for it?

I'll say this for myself, I had the nerve, then—for a moment, anyway—heading south to the airport in an endless stream of traffic, people coming or going—why? where?—the procession I've resisted joining since coming west.

The procession of the hopeful, I guess you could call it. Those people who still want to be seen and heard.

I got to New York as though the trip was familiar, was met by a limousine and rode that, too, as though it was my way. He took me to a midtown hotel, a rookery where the noise never stopped, even at four AM: televisions blaring, toilets flushing, footsteps in the hall outside my room. A baboon palace, it seemed to me, stuffed full of the eternally hopeful. I didn't get to sleep till a gray slice of dawn slid under the heavy curtains, and a machine voice on the telephone woke me an hour later.

The same limousine driver, gaunt and pale, was waiting for me at the curb. The gaseous New York dawn was breaking, purple and gold: June, and still a hint of freshness in the air.

I climbed in, made my manners, and got a look at myself in the rear-view mirror: I looked like death warmed over, plaster-colored from the noisy night I'd spent tossing on a mattress that felt too thick and a pillow that felt too thin and smelled of other people's breath. I sat back and relaxed, knowing they'd fix me up at the studio.

As soon as I was ushered into the holding area backstage, I knew I was in trouble. I went around shaking hands and saying how-de-do, and the first person whose paw I gripped was a transvestite in one of those fright wigs, and the next was the man I used to see at the library in Santa Fe, wearing his pink percale dress; and then there was what appeared to be a female giantess from Colorado who was a tractor pull champion; and finally I got to a monkeyish survivalist in all his camouflage gear.

"You don't look like you belong here," he said, grinning at me, as though it was an honor to look strange.

I sat down, and we started chattering, trying to reassure ourselves. "I think you look cool," the giantess told me, putting a ham fist on each of her knees. "After all, it's a free world"—which I think she knew was a lie.

The survivalist offered to show me his cartridge belt but I told him not to disturb his getup.

I could tell they had all come from a long way away and had probably spent the same kind of night I had, tossing in a strange bed, wondering if they were finally going to have a chance to tell their stories.

"I know a girl in Tulsa who got a book contract out of this," the transvestite told me. "She was on a victim show and one of the other women, I think she had cigarette burn tattoos, got a public service video out of it."

"I just want a chance to have my say," I told him.

So we droned and grinned until a woman with a clipboard came and took us away, one by one, to be made up for the television lights.

While I waited my turn, the transvestite, whose name was Candy, told me her friend had won the Applause-o-Meter contest on her show and that was what had brought about the book contract. "She's working on it, now," he told me, and I thought how much better he looked (in spite of the red fright wig) in his leotard and black net tights than he would have dressed in jeans and T-shirt to work construction, which was what he told me he did.

When it was my turn to be made up, the woman with the clipboard passed right by me.

"Wait a minute," I said. "Aren't you going to do something about me?"

"You're not on the list."

"I need all the help I can get, Miss. I'm pale as death, hardly slept a wink last night."

"I don't know what to do for you," she said, not looking at me.

"Just the same as you did for her," I said, pointing at the giantess, who had come back all peaches and cream.

The woman looked startled.

I reassured her. "I always use plenty of mascara and eye shadow when I'm heading for the clubs."

"I'll have to ask," she said and hurried off, leaving me with the tail end of an uncertain smile.

"Why do you bother?" the giantess asked, offering me a piece of gum, which I refused. "I tell you I could do without all the fussing."

I pointed out that even the survivalist had his bristle powdered; it wasn't a question of sex, just of trying to look our best under those hot lights. "I'm thinking of the folks back home," I told her, then wondered exactly who I meant.

"You got family?" she asked, cracking gum in that big jaw; it sounded like firecrackers going off in a cave.

"You think I'm all alone in the world? Do I look that pitiful?"

She looked at me, big bald eyes an inch from my face, like she was studying an insect through a magnifying glass. "You look okay to me, but then, I wouldn't know."

"Wouldn't know what?"

She turned those headlights on me again. "Wouldn't know what people like you expect."

"You think I'm related to my own kind?"

It was such a strange thought, I started laughing. She turned away, firing off those crackers, hoping to get rid of me before I said something worse.

I wasn't going to let her off so easy. "I've got a son who'll be watching," I told her, wishing it was so, and she gaped at me again. "Listen," I blurted out, "I like a good fuck as well or better than you do."

It was probably lucky they called us then to go and sit on stage.

A hustling female arranged us in a semicircle of chairs, shoving us like we were children; the show was live, and she was fussing about the time we were taking to settle ourselves. I got a seat on the end.

Then Bill Christian walked in, with his mike. He looked us over, and his blue eyes made me nervous; they had a glare like my Uncle Dudley's, the preacher back in the Purchase. I've seen that shade of blue on convicts and con men: so bright you're blinded by it and can't see what's going on.

The mike seemed to be forming an opinion of its own as it gaped at us out of his hand.

Bill glanced at some sheets of information he had on a clipboard, and I wondered what in the name he had on me. The printed slip with my name at the top was my first clue: we weren't being put on prime-time TV to tell our own stories. Bill Christian was going to let us know who we were.

The lights were as fierce as June sun in the desert, and with Bill prowling up and down in front of me, I felt trapped in a hot cage. I was trying to figure how I could pull myself out of the situation with least harm done when I looked through the glare and saw a bunch of women sitting out there: our audience, waiting.

I saw red sweaters and suits and skirts and dresses; they were dressed to the nines in the flaming red that's supposed to look good on TV—had ransacked closets or gone on shopping sprees to find the matching accessories, high-heeled red pumps nobody outside the cities wears anymore and hard-looking red purses with straps. There they were, excited and happy, waiting for their own quick-as-a-wink appearance on national television; I was sure each one of them had a question prepared, one sure to hook Bill Christian's wandering attention.

I caught a smile, and a wink, and a nod: my kind, telling me they were there for me, just the way they've always been, on the dance floor and off. The heat of the lights was raising the sweet and salty smell that makes me think of the clubs: women dressed and perfumed and prepared for anything, and sweating through the preparations.

I winked and nodded back at them—Bill was grilling the survivalist with a news story I'm sure the guy believed was buried in some Rocky Mountain newspaper file—and I knew I had a little time before it was my turn to be embarrassed. At least there was nothing in my past like taking federal subsidies from a government I was trying to blow up, although the point seemed kind of puny, to me; the guy was a survivalist of another stripe, I thought, doing whatever he needed to keep body and soul together, and if somebody would pay attention to him because he wore fatigues and carried a carbine and spouted that the world was run by a secret conclave of scientists and Jews, why, that was just a more original way of qualifying for the dole.

Bill Christian came to me next.

It wasn't what I expected.

Some sidekick must have gone around Santa Fe, asking questions, and the answers—anonymous, of course—made up the profile somebody had composed. (Useful word, profile; it means half a face.) I didn't believe—still don't—I have an enemy in the world, but there are always people around who'll spew out a mouthful of suspicions, if they think that's what's wanted and they don't have to give their names.

More people had noticed me at the clubs than I'd realized, and they'd come to their own conclusions.

Bill had found someone who claimed I was a known lesbian, and another who swore I was a cross-dresser who wore suit and tie during the day (in Santa Fe?), and some poor woman had been led to say I'd mauled her on the dance floor at the La Fonda. I knew then, and not for the first time, why men sometimes act thin-skinned; who can stand up to a lifetime of other people's expectations?

I guessed right away who'd said I'd mauled her, though I certainly wasn't going to talk about it into Bill Christian's hungry little face. It was a woman I met a while back who didn't know how to twirl. I'd refused (politely, I'd hoped) to dance a second time with her, because in Country-Western, you're stuck in a pretty monotonous pattern if you can't break out of it every now and then with a twirl.

I was stuck in a monotonous pattern that morning, buried under layers of metal and concrete while Bill tried to ram his version of who I was down my throat.

"I've been married ten years," I told him, thinking that would bring him up short, but instead it gave him a chance to talk about some statistic citing the number of people who don't know their partner's sexual identity.

As though my sexual identity has anything to do with the fact I like to lead!

"You might as well say I'm weird because I still like the taste of bacon," I told him. That got a laugh from my friends.

He went blathering on, and I decided to speak to those women, all in red—my friends in the audience.

"I married the first time when I was twenty-one," I told them, "too young to know any better." That drew a chuckle; we all remember those times. "I had my first and only child, my boy Buddy, when I was all of twenty-two. I did what we all did, back then—" I said this directly into Bill Christian's face and he shut up, for a minute. "I went the way we all go—women, that is. Girls. We don't have much choice in the matter, as I see it. Nature needs us to carry on the race. So we start out wanting love and babies so bad we're glad to accept a bargain. I accepted a bad bargain, though I didn't know it at the time—we never do. It took me most of the rest of my life to find that out."

Bill tried to interrupt me then but I rode right over him, powered by the bright looks of all those women in red.

"You don't believe me," I told him, "look at the women in your life." I knew he was married to a movie star who gave it all up (whatever that might happen to have been) to stay home with the kiddies. "Can you tell me truthfully (cross your heart and hope to die) you ever knew a woman older than twenty or younger than forty didn't want love and babies? You call that a choice? Or a woman over forty who's willing to make the same bargain?"

"There's a tragedy out there," he said, "time running out for all you gals who thought you could have everything—"

"The tragedy is all those ways to make women have babies, all those devices, when maybe it's the Man all the time saying, Choose another dream."

He saw he was losing it, so he asked if I actually believed in God.

"Sure do," I said.

A woman in the front row jumped up to testify, and Bill rushed his mike down to her. I think he was glad to get out of my way before I started talking more about God.

"I know I went to extremes," this pretty pale middle-aged woman was telling us, grasping at the mike Bill kept just out of her reach. "I let those fertility doctors tear my life apart. I almost lost my husband over it. He didn't want to be told when to do it, what position, he likes to make up his own mind on things like that."

"Maybe the Man's against it," I said. "There're too many children as it is." It was hard right then to remember the Man saying, Feed my lambs.

That triggered an uproar Bill was glad to escape by turning to the giantess.

She was nice enough to nod and smile, agreeing with the story he'd invented for her; maybe her real story was even worse, or she didn't know she had one. Bill gave her the usual: childhood abuse, hormones forced on her as a punishment until she sprang full-blown into his definition of a freak.

I knew then we were all there to prove Bill's definition of a freak, although he would never have used that word.

After a few more minutes, he started taking telephone calls, and the first one concerned me.

"I just want to say I admire your spunk," Heidi in Oklahoma boomed.

"What exactly do you mean?" Bill wanted to know.

I didn't need to hear the answer.

"A lot of women want to lead," Heidi told him, still booming like a priest in a cathedral, "but we hide it because we know men don't like it."

"How do you know that?" Bill asked.

The audience started laughing then—howling, more like it; I had them prepared, and Bill Christian for the first time in his made-for-TV life looked a little annoyed.

"I accept all kinds of behavior in my wife," he told us, expecting us to quiet down and ask respectfully, "Like what?" Then he could have spread out his wares as a sympathizer. But the audience was in full cry now, and they didn't stop to ask if his wife required breakfast in bed or a smart slap on the bottom before she'd come.

We didn't know, and we didn't care; we were talking among ourselves, now, in twos and threes. I'd climbed down off the platform and gone to join in, although some busybody was trying to herd me back to my place.

That's when I developed my special signature.

Those women wanted me to autograph anything they could find, calendars and planners and stick-on notes, even a flattened-out tissue. I started off signing my full name, but that got boring fast, and I began to devise something more playful.

After a few tries, I came up with a boot shaped more or less out of my three initials, with some curlicues added. I signed myself that way for a long time afterwards, whenever the occasion arose:

Melanie O'Bannon Walker (shaped like a boot).

2

I paid for spiting Bill Christian, paid in money I couldn't afford. When I got back to Santa Fe, my husband Buck was gone.

I'd driven my pickup faster than the seventy-five mile-an-hour limit on the throughway north from Albuquerque, and when I topped the rise at La Bajada, it wasn't a ragged Indian boy I saw but my own cozy town, spread out in twinkling lights.

I roared down the hill, my little Ford showing what she's made of, and whirled along Cerrillos Road past the car dealerships and the big hotels, dust and litter flying, the sky over the Sangre de Cristo mountains bruise-purple, showing the first star. All I wanted was to get home to Buck, sit on his lap and tell him about my adventure, maybe open a beer.

I turned into the Land of Enchantment Trailer Park, slowed down, finally, for the speed bumps, and parked next to the big Wilderness we've been living in for the past five years. Right away, I saw the awning was gone.

Buck cranks that awning out the first hot day of summer, and we set our folding chairs under it. The nights I'm not dancing, we sit there for an hour before bed; after ten years, there's not much to talk about, never was, maybe. Words aren't what count, anyway. Now and then Buck steps into the Wilderness to fetch us each another cold beer, and sometimes he brings out popcorn or pretzels, too. Generally, that's our dinner, unless we decide to climb into my truck and drive down the road to the Sonic for two old-time hamburgers served on a tray that clips to the door.

Now the awning was gone.

I unlocked the Wilderness door, and the entire thing vibrated when I stepped in.

"Buck!" I called down the hallway that leads to our bedroom.

There's nowhere much to hide, in the Wilderness.

Then I started in to wait, figuring he might have gone out for something to eat. The refrigerator's too small to hold food for regular meals, and besides, I don't like to cook. But all the time I knew Buck would never in his right mind have gone off when he knew I was on my way home.

I sat outside on the metal step; what in the world had he done with our folding chairs? We've used them all over the West, even carting them down to the beach in Oregon a couple of summers ago; we take a road trip once a year, going someplace we haven't seen. Buck lives off his Social Security and savings, plus my wage and tips, and the only fixed part of our life is my job and my two or three nights a week dancing at the clubs. Other than that, we are both free in a way we never imagined when Buck was foreman on million-dollar haciendas going up on the ridges and couldn't miss a day of work without throwing the project off schedule.

When it came on to full dark, I went inside the Wilderness and opened the clothes closet; every stitch he had was gone.

I sat down then and cried. Buried my face in the daisy-print pillowcases I'd bought with my last paycheck and howled. I missed those clothes almost more than I missed the man. I knew every article Buck wore from the day I met him, broke down by the Taos road, thumbing for a ride. I'd hauled his checked flannel shirts and white T's and patched jeans (not my patches; some other lady in Buck's long past must have had a special ability I don't claim) to the Laundromat so many times those man-shaped pieces of cloth felt like my own skin: worn down and soft, the way Buck himself felt when I held him in my arms. Buck, who'd insisted on marrying me when living together was going far enough, the way I saw it; Buck, who even though he was deep asleep and snoring when I came home from the clubs, never failed to turn over and kiss me goodnight.

After I'd cried myself out—my first good cry in years—I called Buck's sister Fern in Tulsa.

It was late by then, and I woke her. Fern tried to be helpful, but what could she say except she hadn't seen or heard from Buck since he called to wish her happy birthday last January?

I went back to the Wilderness and sat on the step.

Jean and Marty next door were having one of their midnight go-arounds, fucking or fighting, it sounds pretty much the same, and I remembered how Buck would grin when we heard them going at it, and nothing I could say would wipe that grin off his face.

The first time I saw him, thumbing on the Taos road, he dropped his hand when he glimpsed me, a woman driving alone, not likely to pick up a grizzled guy with a backpack, and it nearly dark.

So I stopped my truck because this man, this stranger, seemed to think I'd be afraid.

"Why'd you drop your hand?" I asked him when he was settled, beat-up backpack on his knees. I needed to know if something about me looked that feminine.

"Women don't generally stop for me," he said, sounding West Texas.

Which was about all the conversation we had, driving down to Santa Fe. I felt no need to tell him I wasn't like all those pretty women afraid of their own shadows—the kind that gape at me, now, when I ask them to dance.

I let him out at the corner of the Paseo and Washington Avenue, next to the rose-red Masonic temple; from there he could make his way to the Plaza, buy something to eat at the Greek's. I never expected to see him again, didn't even know his name.

He turned up a couple of nights later at Rita's, where I work. As soon as he saw me, he headed in my direction, and I thought, This man has nerve.

He sat down in my section, ordered a cup of "the real stuff," drank about half of it and left me a five-dollar tip.

I went after him with the money. "You don't owe me this."

He was standing in line at the cashier. "I don't like to be beholden," he said, and his blue eyes flashed at me, bright in his shabby, worked-over face.

And I never remembered till now the man has pride.

Marty and Jean had come to the end of whatever they were trying to accomplish in their camper, and the trailer park was quiet. Late as it was, I knew I couldn't face that bed at the end of the Wilderness, with the quilted cover Buck never liked—so many roses—and the vanity mirror that's seen too much. I took some change out of the coffee mug on the dinette table—Buck always keeps it well supplied—and went back down to the payphones. There was one person I could still call: my best friend.

Doris was asleep, but she woke up when she heard my voice.

"I've got to see you," I said.

"Get right on over."

I headed out Cerrillos toward Madrid. Doris works the same shift at Rita's as me; she lives with her son on the edge of the mesa in a little adobe she bought with the money from her divorce.

The city lights faded behind me, and I rolled down my window and breathed in the high desert: piñon, tangy as creosote, and dry red dirt, and sage. Big soft clouds were climbing the night sky; the Sandias heaved up black near Albuquerque, blocking that city's lights.

I knew, even then, I was in my right place. Not the clapboard hen roost in Gloucester where I'd lived in my twenties, working the summer trade; not the dorm in Tucson where I'd managed to survive a year of college; not the little town in the Purchase where my mother raised me with only the Bible and Pilgrim's Progress to help her, but here, on the high desert at the southern toe of the Rockies, the land where heartbreak begins.

It began for me that night.

I cried myself silly, sitting at Doris' kitchen table at one AM—and we both had the first shift, next day.

"What makes you think he won't come back when he's worked his way through this?" Doris asked. "He's run off before, hasn't he?"

"Restless, or chasing some woman. This is different. Did you see my TV show?"

She nodded, pinching her lips. Doris at night looks bone-yellow and brittle, not someone to dispute with over a lukewarm cup of tea; by day, in make-up and *señorita* uniform (short red dress, white apron; Rita's depends on tourists), she's saucy and wise. All of that had boiled away now, and I knew why I liked her: the bone strength that doesn't soften, doesn't change.

"I saw it. Dumb thing to do," she said, shaking her head. "Very, very stupid."

"I got carried away."

"You were showing off, Mel. I expected you to get up and demonstrate how you lead some woman through an underarm turn."

"I told you, I got carried away."

"Think what Buck saw: his wife, dolled up in boy clothes, talking about how a woman feels in her arms."

"Buck's known all along—"

"Not on national television."

"You sound like you're telling me I deserve him leaving." Something started up in me, a redness kin to rage.

"You didn't think about the consequences."

"There never were any consequences, before. He didn't say anything when I told him I was going."

"Told him?"

I took a breath. "I don't usually ask permission."

"There you are."

"Buck knows I like to lead," I told her.

"It's different when a million people know, too. Think how you'd feel if Buck went on some talk show and told about his other women."

"I wouldn't care. I know all about them, anyway." Not true, but close enough to it.

Doris smiled. Then she stood up, tightening the tie on her blue chenille robe. "I'm not going to argue with you, Mel. Just think about what I said." She carried her cup to the sink. "I put a pillow and blankets on the couch. It gets cold, toward dawn."

The rest of that night I tossed and turned, dreams I didn't know I could muster weaving through my head. At six, when I'd finally dropped off, Doris woke me with a cup of her terrible coffee; we both needed to dress and go to work.

I thanked her for her kindness and drove back home.

I expected to find Buck, or at least a message from him, but there was nothing: no note pinned to the door or waiting under the rock from Diablo Canyon we use as a message-holder and key-keeper. No sign of him at all.

I didn't have time to start crying again.

That day passed in a daze. Luckily for me, the restaurant wasn't crowded. I could space out, imagine alternatives to what was facing me: Buck back, still loving me, or me somehow getting over whatever his problem was.

I attended to my few customers, so used to the routine I didn't need to think about it, and claimed my paycheck at the end of my shift. There was a deduction I didn't understand, and I knew how near the edge I was when I heard myself raising my voice with the manager, Mrs. Lopez.

Doris heard, too, and came over. "Melanie's under a lot of strain," she said.

Mrs. Lopez was glaring at me over her shoulder, hand on the swinging door to the kitchen. She glanced at Doris; they were good friends, sometimes went to the pueblo casino to play the slots on Sunday night.

"She'd better keep her voice down around me," Mrs. Lopez said, and Doris hustled me out.

"Let's get something to eat," she said, but I told her I wanted to go straight home and change.

"You're not going out," she told me, giving me a look.

"I always hit Club Alegria on Friday night."

"Not this Friday, you don't. What if Buck takes it into his head to come home and you're not there?"

"He'd know where to find me."

"You're stubborn as a mule, Melanie. I'm starting to wonder why Buck put up with it as long as he did," Doris said, going to her car.

I didn't feel stubborn, standing there on the gravel, watching her charge off.

I cared about Buck, but I couldn't let that stop me. I needed to go to the darkness and the music and the feel of a woman in my arms; my spirit was wilting, and I knew only the Two-Step could save me from giving out altogether—at least for a while.

I showered and put on my blacks (as I call them; I don't own a piece of ordinary clothes that's black, just my dancing duds) and shined my boots, sitting on the trailer step. Buck used to watch me do that, sucking on his cigarette, and I wondered for the first time what he'd been thinking.

We tried dancing together once or twice, years ago, but it didn't work. We're both strong, well-built, almost the same height, and when we stepped out on the dance floor, we seemed to lock. When we finally did more, it was like two heavy wooden crates bumping along. We decided dancing was one thing we were not going to do together.

That's when I started going to the clubs alone.

We never talked about that, either.

I put on my boots and went back in the trailer to check myself in the mirror. I liked what I saw. My long-sleeved black ruffled shirt was tucked in my belt, and the red bandanna I'd knotted inside my collar looked fresh and sharp. My concho belt (Buck gave it to me our first Christmas) couldn't measure up to what the tourists wear, but I like its plainness: silver disks with a pie crust rim, strung on a narrow piece of black leather. The crease in my jeans was sharp, and I'd learned how to tuck them into my boots so there were no wrinkles below the knee. Underneath, I had on pantyhose and my push-up bra.

I combed my short, orangey hair with my fingers, and set my black Stetson (Buck again, our second Christmas) flat on my head. Then I was ready.

Going out to my pickup, I thought how it was the way I wore my hat that made the difference. Most girls cock a Stetson, give it a flirta-tious angle, but that hat's meant for business, and I always wear mine flat, like I have some branding in mind.

I roared out of the trailer park, sailing across the speed bumps, raising dirt and litter and setting the dog chained outside a big Win-nebago into a frenzy of barking.

I enjoyed that.

I turned on Airport Road and again on Aqua Fria, going a little too fast, and when I heard my poor old tires squealing, I looked in the rear-view mirror and wondered what I was up to:

Fifty-five years old, fresh out of a husband, and already hitting the road.

It's Friday night, I told that frowning stranger in the mirror. I always go dancing on Friday night. What am I supposed to do, sit in the Wilderness and cry?

Buck wouldn't want me to do that.

My face in spite of everything I'd done for it looked bleached, and I remembered catching a glimpse of myself, coming off the TV set in New York, flushed so I looked almost like the girl I never was or even wanted to be.

Maybe that was what bothered Buck, more than me bragging about dancing with women: the way I'd enjoyed the attention, the way I'd turned into somebody I never was and didn't want to be.

I pulled into the Alegria's parking lot and stopped under the big arc light, my only precaution against walking back to my car alone, later. The Alegria used to be known for rough carryings-on, but things have changed since Father Garcia leads the combo; most of the crowd are his parishioners at San Isidro up the road.

The little guy who takes your five dollars at the door bobbed his head at me, and José who shines shoes and boots at the back called out hello. They both know me from way back; I'm one of the few women who remembers to give the little guy, Pedro, an extra dollar now and then, and I'm a pretty frequent customer of José's, sitting up high on his chair while he busies himself around my boots.

I waded into the darkness and found the last seat at the ledge along the dance floor, which is for women alone looking for partners; couples and groups sit at the tables.

Right away I knew it was going to be my kind of night.

Father Garcia was in the middle of a Meringue, playing keyboard with his left hand and leading his three musicians with his right, and Jerry had the rattles flying. The floor was thick with couples, and I waved at a few people I knew; the turning lights caught skirts and belt buckles and earrings, glanced off a bald pate or two, lit up some amazing curls. Over at the pool tables, four or five guys were concentrating on their game, ignoring the music, and the servers were threading through the tables, carrying drinks from the bar. The fine thick darkness was lit with colored flashes from the turning lights on the dance floor, and the air smelled rich with sweat and perfume and popcorn and beer and cigarette smoke. The sounds were the prancing of the Meringue, the dry rattles, the pump-pump-pump of Father Garcia's left hand on his keyboard and the heavy breathing of people doing what they do best: holding each other and moving to music.

The ledge had ten or twelve chairs lined up, and a woman was sitting on each one, fingers wrapped around a glass, eyes on the dance floor. Here and there, a dress boot was tapping out the rhythm, not impatient, not over-eager, just waiting for the chance to be beckoned or led onto the floor: to move.

That's what I love about women: that patient, certain waiting.

I took my place at the ledge, the only space left.

The woman to my left glanced at me, looked away, looked back: "These places are reserved for women."

I smiled at her. "What do I have to do to prove I belong here?"

She tried to look shocked, laughed instead. "That get-up—"

"I see by my get-up that I am a cowboy."

She laughed again.

"Care to dance?" I asked, taking her hand, which she'd placed on the table between us.

Once I have the hand, I usually have the woman.

She was saying things, but following along behind.

"I dress this way to improve the ratio," I said, to keep her smiling.

Stepping down onto the dance floor was like stepping into a well: swirl, reflections, colors. No one moved aside to let us in, but somehow we found our place.

I hooked my arm around this lady and led us both into the swirl.

Right away I knew I was in luck. She had that airiness and balance, felt the way I imagine a bird feels, perching on a swaying limb: sure, yet delicate, the little talons barely touching.

Now she was turning under my arm like a bright little top, flourishing her skirt—a *señorita* on a poster. She was smiling and whirling as she'd looked forward to doing when she put on her cherry-red lipstick and hung shiny purple hoops in her ears.

I was her dream come true, for that minute, anyway.

"I haven't seen you here before," I said.

"I'm just visiting"—the standard reply when they don't know whether or not they want to give you their telephone number. Not that I take them, but a few have tried.

Her nose was level with my collar bone, and I was looking down at the white part in her black hair. She wore it the old-fashioned way, pulled back and fastened with pins. The bit of her neck and shoulder I could see was white and smooth as a beach-worn pebble; she wasn't as young as she looked, but she'd taken good care of herself.

"You're good," I said on our second turn around the floor.

"Thanks." She looked up at me. "You always take the man's part?"

"Yes."

"Why?"

I sighed. It seemed so simple to me, so complicated to other people. "I like to lead."

She nodded like she understood, which of course she didn't.

"Haven't I seen you somewhere?"

"Only on national TV." I couldn't hold it back, though right away I knew I should have.

"That show!" She was goggle-eyed now.

"Don't tell anybody." But she was already running to her friends.

After that a few people started asking questions: What was it like? What did they say? I wish I could have told them the way the pillow smelled in that New York hotel.

I sat down to study the possibilities, and it occurred to me what I loved about leading was the order. On the floor, I always knew what was going to happen: I chose. There was some order to the rest of my life, as well—working, good times with Buck—but under that something infernal was always rumbling. Hell fire, I'd have called it. Buck's temper? Yes, that—although he wasn't any worse than others I've known, in that department. But the rumbling was more than a raised voice now and then. It was the end coming on, like a freight train. The end of it all, before I even knew what that all was. At least when I was leading I felt like I was clear of the track.

Next I decided to try one of two women sitting at a table near the door. She'd been looking at me like she knew me, because of the show.

She barely reached my chest, which makes leading awkward. I had to rely too much on steering her with my arms.

"You're jerking me," she complained when we launched into a Mambo.

"Sorry." I took a firmer hold of her, trying to rotate her with my body, but she pulled back.

"You're that woman that was on the show!"

"Never pretended to be anything else."

She turned on her heel and stalked off the dance floor.

I guess being known has its downside, too.

I went back to my spot on the ledge. The dark-haired lady, my first partner, was waiting for me.

"Care to?" she asked.

"Sure."

I could feel those two women at the table near the door burning my back with their eyes.

Lucky for me, it was a Country Waltz.

We started those small circles, and then I turned her out into Promenade; Shadow came next—my left arm across her shoulders, her back against my chest. She knew how.

"You a lesbian?" she asked when I turned her back into dance position.

The floor was crowded, and I was concentrating on guiding her through. "Not especially," I said.

"It's either yes or no."

"I've never tried it, or wanted to, with a woman, so how would I know?"

"I haven't either," she said, going into an underarm turn. "Don't think I ever will," she added when we were circling again.

"Half the women I dance with ask me that," I told her, "and the other half are probably wondering. Fact is, I'm married."

"To a man?"

"Nothing else is legal, as far as I know."

"Well," she said, and now we were back in Shadow, "I admire you."

Strange words. I don't believe I'd ever heard them before.

"I pay the price," I said.

"Which is?"

"My husband just left me."

"For good?"

"He goes off from time to time, but this feels different."

"You dancing this way got something to do with it?"

"Maybe. I think more that show."

"You shamed him," she said.

We were coming to the end of the set, and Father Garcia was getting ready to take his break. I didn't want to spend fifteen minutes talking about what was wrong between me and Buck, especially since I wasn't sure yet what it was.

"Do you dance with your husband the way you dance with

women?" she asked on our way back to our seats.

"Buck doesn't like to dance."

"If he did, would you take the man's part?"

"He wouldn't let me," I told her when she'd settled herself with a flourish of red skirts and white petticoats.

Father Garcia passed us, and I reached up to shake his hand. I didn't need to remind him who I am; he has the good shepherd's eye for each sheep in his flock.

"Haven't seen you at mass in a while," he told me. He's tall as a lighthouse, with a big polished dome of a head.

"I went to New York."

"So I heard."

"Did anybody see my show?"

"Quite a few. I heard comments. You've got some explaining to do."

"They've seen me dancing before," I said.

"They never heard you talk about it," he said, passing along; there were hands waving at him, down the line.

Then they put on the taped music, and everybody got up again to dance. It was Salsa, hot and loud.

Buck wouldn't let me, I'd told her. That stuck in my craw. It never had come to me like that before—the meaning of my leading. It wasn't just Buck. The world wouldn't let me.

I went across the room to ask an older woman I'd spotted, sitting with a group of friends.

She wasn't much of a dancer, this lady. The music was a slow rumba, and I explained the basic step-close-step to her and even told her a little about Cuban motion. She was about my height, nicely dressed, with a pretty head of gray hair; I figured she was one of those late divor-cées with a whole lifetime behind her who come to Santa Fe to see what it is they've missed, raising four children in a Dallas suburb.

We danced four or five times, and she even started to move

her hips a little, like her spine had come unfused. Marriage locks most women at the hips, I've noticed. When I felt her start to soften, I thought about warm water and soft sand and summertime—all still waiting for me when I hold a woman in my arms.

I don't know why life isn't soft. That's one of the first lessons everybody has to learn. Hard is the way we have to go, and hard we get to be. Maybe dancing softens me because I don't need words; leading is touching. The woman gets it, or doesn't, moves, or doesn't. Either way, there's nothing to say.

Words chip. You know they do, I know they do. Music and moving don't chip. They glide. And I lead that glide with my belly and thighs. Pushing trays at work, rocking under Buck at night—that, too: belly and thighs. But not to music.

After our fifth dance, she told me she had to leave, and I gave her my little bow and thanked her for the pleasure from the bottom of my heart.

The stars were coming out through a thick band of clouds when I left the Alegria; there'd been a storm while I was dancing, and the roads were streaming. I knew some folks would have trouble getting home where arroyos had flooded and washed out roads, and would probably end up spending the night in their trucks.

I was driving too fast, singing at the top of my lungs, and even when I pulled into the trailer court and headed for our slot, I didn't shut my mouth.

Then I saw Buck's pickup, parked alongside the Wilderness.

— 3 —

"We might as well begin with bed, that's where we'll end up," Buck said. He'd been sitting in the dinette for I don't know how long, not even opening a beer. He had on clothes I'd never seen, new jeans and a tan windbreaker over a Route 66 T-shirt.

"All right by me," I said.

"You and I can talk each other out of anything."

"We've come pretty close, a few times."

He took off his windbreaker.

"Where'd you get that?" I asked. It looked expensive.

"Layors to catch meddlars."

I stood up, too. In the florescent light, we must have looked pale, gawky, two aging amateur fighters in a homemade ring, circling to throw the first punch.

"Come here," he said.

I went.

He took hold of my wrist and pulled me toward the bedroom.

It wasn't leading. It was pulling. Yanking.

I uncurled his fingers from around my wrist. "I don't want to be dragged, Buck."

He turned, cramped in the small doorway. "You always want to lead."

"That's why I dance with women—no other reason."

He put one arm around me and winched me through the door.

"You knew I like to lead," I said, sitting on the bed. "I've told you a thousand times."

"Sounds different, in front of all those people. Sounds . . ."

"Spit it out, Buck."

He was kneeling beside me. "Sounds butch."

"You know I'm not."

"I don't know anything about you, Mel, not for sure. I was thinking on the way back here—I drove nearly a thousand miles—you never did want to marry me."

"You persuaded me."

"Why? You don't want to cook, stay home."

"I wanted to spend time with you.

"Me, too," he said. "Still do." He got up, dusting his knees.

"Where'd you go?" I asked.

He looked away. "I was thinking, all that time, we live our life together, pretty much, but I never know what goes on inside your head." He sat on the edge of the bed, his hands hanging between his knees. "You could be anything."

"I waited ten years to hear you say that. Thank you, Buck."

"Now, what kind of crazy—"

"You still love me?"

"Yes."

"Even though you don't know for sure who or what I am?"

"That's the hell of it." He sighed. Then he shook his head, and I half expected to hear harness jingling. "I don't want to be told on television who my wife is."

"You want to just know."

He nodded, looking down. I saw the creases in the side of his neck; his skin was rough and red, like clay. I figured he'd gone south to Mexico, where he had some compadres from another life. "If we'd ever had kids—" he said.

"That would have settled me down?"

"Maybe."

"I thought we weren't going to talk."

He leaned back on his elbows. "Now we've started, I don't see how we can stop. There're some things—"

"We can stop, anytime." I started to work that new T-shirt out of his belt. He sighed, then reached over, like always, and flipped on the radio.

Bonnie, wailing.

He was starting to say something but I pressed my palm over his mouth. Then for a little while we were babies, lipping, sucking. The sweetness of that well-worn way: I thought there was a chance we could slip right back into it.

"You hear me? You hear me good?" he whispered in my ear, and I felt his breath stir the fringes of my orange hair.

"Yes," I said.

"You stay home, now. In the evenings. No more gallivanting to the clubs."

"Oh, Buck," I said, "If you loved me, you'd be proud of me."

His big chest came down on my breasts; I always love that first touch of his skin on my nipples—it takes my breath away. I wrapped my legs around him, knowing how he loves the feel of my strong thighs.

"You stay home," he said.

Buck's a big man, and when I'm not ready, I can't accommodate him.

"You want me to lick you?" he asked.

"What I don't want is to have to make promises. I'm not willing to give up who I am."

He reared back, staring at me. "Don't turn this into some kind of test, Mel."

"You don't want to do this," he said a minute later, coming up from between my legs.

"Not if it's going to cost me a promise I can't keep." I wanted it, I wanted him. But the price was too high.

He sat back, reached a pack of cigarettes out of his pants pocket, cupped his hands, lighting up, and I wondered if the new woman was already after him to quit. I'd tried that for a few years, then given up. "Can't a man just want to spend some time with you?"

"Sure," I said, putting my hand on his shoulder. "But take me like I am. I don't ask you to change."

He growled something, inhaling.

"What?"

"Loyalty." He coughed, spat out a fiber of tobacco.

"Is that all you want?"

"Not all, but it'll do, for a start."

"A start, after all this time?"

"Something's got to change, Mel."

I didn't have anything to say.

He was still hard. He'd pulled the sheet up over himself, but I could see. Bodies tend to tell the truth.

I touched him. "Let's leave all that for later."

This time, I was ready for him.

What does that say about me? You'll have to guess.

The truth under the truth—and one doesn't contradict the other—is that he wanted me, and I wanted him. Nothing was settled. It never is. Buck's anger was just this side of dangerous; that lent what we were doing an edge.

Afterwards I made him coffee.

He had a pillow propped up against the headboard, and the back of his head was matching the smudge on the wall.

I said, "Now tell me who you've been with."

"I went on down to Juarez."

"Where'd you stay?"

"Stopped in El Paso at the El Presidente. It was too late to cross the bridge so I slept till nine, had breakfast by the pool. You remember those burritos, from the big buffet they spread?"

"I do."

"Then I went across the street to the shopping center, watched the kids ice skate for a while. I decided to try it—"

"What!"

"Never skated in my life. They didn't have rental skates big enough, so I went ahead and bought myself a pair. They're in the pickup now."

"I never would have believed it."

"I felt like I needed to move. And there was music—that old-time organ.

"I fell down a lot at first, but then I got the hang of it, and I started to fly. Just fly. They had to send somebody to tell me to slow down."

I could see it: Buck slashing the ice as he bore down on crowds of kids that separated to let him through.

"All the way down to El Paso to go ice skating," I said. It wasn't what I wanted to say. I wanted to congratulate him.

I also wanted to sit on his lap and tuck my chin into his shoulder, smell him, taste his skin.

He didn't say anything. I edged up closer. "So what did you do next?"

"Felt so good I bought myself all new clothes, balled up what I had on—underwear, socks, everything—and gave it to the sales clerk."

"I thought those pants were new." Then I had to ask, "You did all that alone?"

"Believe it or not . . ."

"I want to believe it, Buck."

He stubbed out his cigarette in the saucer he keeps by the side of the bed. "I did go out to the bars that night, over in Juarez."

I remembered the strip: early evening, the hawkers out, waving people in to see the decor—cave motif. Most of those clubs are two levels down (no fire laws, south of the border), stalactites made out of plaster hanging from the ceiling, everything dark as the pit and smelling stale.

"You go back to the hotel alone?" I asked.

"Sure."

"You don't have to lie to me, Buck."

He studied me. "That so?"

"I'm the one that has to lie, it looks like. I'm not sure what you did matters, anyway."

"It doesn't." He was glad for a way out. "I was feeling low, you on television making a monkey out of me."

"A sort of pick-me-up?"

"Maybe so," Buck said.

"So we both had our little flings," I said, getting up to put on one of his old shirts. It was nearly one AM, turning cool: time to get some sleep. I checked the alarm. Six would come too soon.

"Wait a minute." Buck was sitting on the side of the bed. "I asked you something."

"I don't make promises, Buck. You ought to know that." I started brushing my hair.

"I'm not going to stand for it anymore," Buck said, leaning back on the bed. "You at those clubs at night."

I threw the hairbrush. It bounced off the wall.

I said, "You always knew who I was, from the start."

"Dancing with women!"

"I let you lead in other ways—"

"You do?"

"Only if I have my turn on the dance floor, pretty regularly." I raised my hand to stop him interrupting. "You can call me anything you want. Just love me the way I am. What kind of love says, This, but not that?"

He reminded me, "You used to cut up something terrible about me going off—"

"I'm not so sure it matters, now." Suddenly I was so tired I had to sit down on the bed.

"I was getting ready to say I won't go off anymore, if you'll cut the dancing," Buck said.

I shrugged, too tired to try. "You always come back to me. Or at least, you always have."

"Aren't you scared I'll fall for somebody else?"

I knew what he meant: my old body, my too-wise old mind.

I shrugged again. What else could I do, or say? Then I noticed my belly, under the T-shirt, sitting like a little sack on my thighs, and I thought, Buck's right, I'm old, now. I'll always be old. Then older.

"You don't care about me," he said, brave the way I hadn't been a while ago.

"I love you, Buck. Maybe not the way you want." I leaned back against the headboard, so tired I wanted to die. "I have to go to work in five hours."

"So if I'd just kept heading south, the way I'd planned, on down to Mexico City . . ."

"What turned you back?"

It was hard for him to say. He got up, said it over his shoulder: "I wanted to see you."

"That's all I want. Turn up the A.C., will you?" I got under the sheet. "And throw me that blanket."

He came with my blue blanket in his arms, and I wondered suddenly what he would have looked like, holding our child.

"I meant what I said, Mel."

"And I told you, no promises I can't keep." I felt like I was carving those words on my bones.

Then he tossed the blanket to me and I pulled it over my head and dived down, deep down, into sleep.

— 4 —

Buck's sister called the next afternoon, hot to tell me.

"I may not want to hear this," I said. I was just home from work, stripping off my clothes to shower, the telephone clamped between my shoulder and ear. There was no sign of Buck in the Wilderness.

"I have a responsibility," Fern said.

"You didn't have a responsibility when we talked two days ago."

"I didn't know about it then. Buck called me this morning."

"He wasn't planning on you hot-footing to me, whatever it is," I warned her.

"I have a responsibility," my sister-in-law repeated.

"Tell, then."

"He's hunted up your son."

I had to sit down. "So it wasn't just the bars and the whores in Juarez."

"Did you really think it was?"

"Well, you don't have to drive all that way, if that's what you're looking for." Then it hit me. "Did Buddy get in touch with him first?"

"Yes. Last week."

So here was another secret.

"Looking for money?"

"Looking for help," Fern said.

I sighed. "What kind of help, this time?"

"I think you better ask Buck," Fern said. There was nothing left in her voice but pity.

"Buck's not here."

"I called you because I care," Fern said.

Like the fool I was, I started to choke up. Fern can be a pain in the ass with her remedies and suggestions; once she told me stewed collard greens would draw the evil out of Buddy, and she also had the nerve to say some kind of root tea fixed menopause—and I never have admitted to the symptoms. But she does care, in her own way. I knew that, and it went right through me.

"I have to hang up now," I said, and then I just sat there and bawled.

It'd been more than a year since I'd seen hide or hair of Buddy, and here he was calling the stepfather he always blamed me for marrying. Where did I come in?

I'd nursed that boy through every ailment in the book including the time he fell off a motorcycle and busted about every bone in his body. I'd hoped for him, dreamed for him, until there wasn't a hope or a dream left. And here he was calling Buck for help, Buck who'd told me years ago, "It's either him or me."

Then I remembered it was my night to dance, and all of that fell away like a suit of rags.

I was almost out the trailer door when I made myself stop. Buck cared how I looked, sometimes more than I did. I went back and fixed my face, found some jeans I'd washed and pressed at an earlier time in my life.

I drove over to Rodeo Nites. Rodeo never has been one of Buck's favorite hangouts (too much dancing, at night—it leaves a flavor in the air), but Dave, my friend and the head bartender, always has his ear to the ground and can hear calamity rattling down the tracks as far away as Lamy.

"Seen Buck?" I asked him. He was behind the bar, and he looked out at me straight and solemn, his eyeglasses glinting.

"That man of yours doesn't come in here, Mel, you know that. Matter of fact, I haven't seen you in a while."

"You play too much Country. When're you going to hire you a good Salsa band?"

"And steal all the folks from the good Father over on Aqua Fria?" He grinned, fingering the ponytail he told me he started growing when he was fourteen. It's gray now. "Come on, I'll buy you a beer."

"I don't drink in the middle of the day."

He opened one for me anyway. "Buck run out on your again?"

"He's found my son," I said, and then for the second time in less than twenty-four hours, I was crying.

Dave passed me a paper napkin. I wiped my eyes and blew my nose.

"I haven't heard you mention the kid in I don't know how long," he said. "How old is he now? Buddy? You never struck me as being mother material, Mel."

"You don't know what you're talking about. I raised him, alone, till he was nineteen. Ten years ago, and hardly a word since."

"What happened?"

"Crack happened. And jail and every kind of craziness. He tore up my place, last time he lived here. Got high and tore the phone out of the wall and smashed every dish in the place. I threw him out—with the help of the police—and after a while he went on down south. To Mexico, or someplace. I get a collect call every now and then—that click, and the voice says, "You will not be charged for this call." I want to say, "I've already been charged."

Dave shook his head. "Crack'll do it, every time. If you have some little thing wrong with your mind, crack'll water it and fertilize it and cultivate it till it's ten feet high."

"I tried everything I could think of. Even tied him to his bed, one time."

"You used to be all the time going down to Madrid. Was that him?"

"Yeah, he laid up there for a while, trying to keep out of the way of a bench warrant."

"Why in the name did Buck go looking for him?"

"Trying to twist my chain. I won't have much time for dancing if Buddy shows up."

"Buck invited him back here?"

I shrugged. "Buddy doesn't need an invitation, but he does need an address."

"Which he didn't have, till now."

"I'm not certain sure Buck gave it to him."

"He was gone when you got back?"

"He turned up, but I didn't know then he'd been down to Mexico after Buddy. Fern clued me."

"Huh, that woman." Dave met her once and drew his own conclusions; she got after him about the smudges on his eyeglasses. "Well, it looks like all you got to do now is worry."

"I worked like a dog to make a decent life for myself," I told him, "found friends, started dancing, fixed things pretty well with Buck. It may not look like a whole lot, but it's the best set-up I've ever had. I can't let Buddy come here and wreck it: police, evictions, druggie friends laying around, breaking in when I'm at work and stealing me bare."

"I don't know how you can stop him coming."

I tried to see myself standing in front of the Wilderness, shaking my fist, threatening to call the police. I tried to see myself staring down my son's despair.

"You're right," I told Dave. "There isn't a single thing I can do."

Then I went on home.

They talk about heartbreak all the time on TV. People crying and carrying on. Well, it's not that way. It's dry. Dry tight throat, crusted lips, splitting nails on spotted hands clenching the steering wheel. Joy on the way out, going to dance, like a desert wind sweeping the scrub. Trouble on the way back—Buck bringing back Buddy—like those far-off storms the Navajo call Walking Rain.

But that's wet, isn't it?

5

Still, I was glad to see Buck's pickup when I got home, even gladder when I opened the door and smelled cooking. Buck was standing in his shorts at the stove, frying up onions and green and yellow peppers. Light played along his tan forearms, flashed off the metal spatula he was using.

"Smells good. I could eat a wolf," I said, stepping in and slinging my purse on the dinette table.

"We're just about out of cooking oil," he said, shoveling pepper slices onto two plates. I was so glad to hear him say "we" I nearly cried.

He put the plates on the table and sat down across from me. His big bare feet nudged mine; I'd slipped off my boots.

"We need to talk some more," I said.

"I'm about out of words," he said, getting up for the salt.

"Then just listen. I need you to understand about my dancing."

He started shaking his head.

"Open your ears, now," I told him. "It doesn't have a thing to do with sex." As I said it, I started to wonder. Sex seemed like a little hard knot of delight that rode somewhere on the big wave of dancing. "It really has to do with giving pleasure."

"I thought that's what you like to get," he growled.

"I do, but that's not the point. The point is to make some woman feel—"

He pushed his plate away. "Come on, now, Mel." He rubbed his mouth on the back of his hand. "I don't want to hear all that."

"All right, then. I'll show you." I stood up and took the broom out of the corner.

A broom's not much to dance with, and at first I thought I wasn't going to be able to do it. Then I remembered the spangled darkness in Alegria, and the fierce stiff spines of some of the women I dance with there, and I laid hold of that broom with a vengeance.

The first step—a Promenade—I was dancing with a stick, a plain stick with a skirt of bristles scraping my bare feet, but then I adjusted my hands on her, giving her a back and shoulders, and took her into a Country Waltz:

Round by the refrigerator, skirting the sink, careful near the edges of the dinette table, then swooping down the hall to the bedroom, twirling at the door, cantering back: that broom was nimble. I'll never look the same way at her and her kin, waiting in dark corners for the music to begin.

At the table, Buck was staring at me.

"You get it?" I asked. "This old stick came to life. It's the same with a woman—" And I wondered suddenly if he'd felt that, or if he'd missed that, with me. I went on, fast. "Her boyfriend doesn't believe in foreplay, she's working sixty hours a week on her feet at Wal-Mart, comes home to the wreck the kids have made of the house, five loads of dirty laundry and nothing for dinner. But when I lead her out on the dance floor"—I grabbed the broom again—"that's all forgotten. Her spine starts to loosen, shoulders droop, hips swivel the way they used to when she was dreaming about making love. It all flows back into her, Buck. That's my gift to her. That's what I can do."

"Can't a man do that?"

I sashayed the broom again. "Maybe, but most men don't want to. (I'm not talking about you, Buck.) They touch a woman"—I showed him, with the broom—"like they're touching a red-hot stove. They don't want any belly-to-belly contact, they're afraid they might get stuck. The broom just floats around them—see?"

"You're talking about the way you feel," Buck said.

"Yes!" And then I was laughing. It never had been so clear before. That broom was me.

I started her on one last figure. Took her into sweetheart position and started prancing toward the door.

Then I saw my son.

Buddy was standing at the door, looking over my head at Buck. "I drove straight up from El Paso," he said.

Buck never said a word.

I opened the screen door. "Come on in."

He brushed past me so close I could smell him: a day on the road, maybe sleeping in his car, probably driving a wreck he bought for five hundred bucks.

He walked to the table, stuck out his hand. Buck took it.

I stood the broom in the corner. "My Lord, Buddy!" He was my child again, my child who'd been bad hurt and somehow gotten over it, without me helping or even knowing. I was so excited I jabbered: "I'm glad to see you, son!"

"Hello, Mom."

He looked thin and worn, older than twenty-nine, and I remembered how knobby and parched his father, Paul, had looked, when I met him in that bar in Taos, a year before Buddy was born.

My heart strings were still hanging out, waiting to be pulled, and Buddy pulled them. His neck looked like a pullet's in the grimy ring of his T-shirt. I wanted to wash that shirt, even iron it; I wanted to cook for him.

Buck stood up and clapped his hands on our shoulders—the boy's and mine, and I knew this was what he wanted: his woman looking with longing at her long-lost son, waiting to wash his dirty shirt.

"Welcome home, Buddy," he said.

"Are you planning on staying?" I asked, steady as I could. "Because if you are, we've got to buy a cot or something,"

"I brought my sleeping bag," he said. "It's out in the car." I wondered if it was the royal-blue sleeping bag he'd saved for when he was fourteen and first fell in love with the mountains; he'd be gone for days at a time, wandering somewhere up near Baldy, or in the Pecos Wilderness, giving me conniptions but always coming back safe and sound.

Buck said, "You can lay it out on the kitchen floor."

I wondered what had turned Buck so accommodating.

"Not this time, I guess," Buddy said.

Then he went to the door, edging by me; when he opened the screen, I looked after him. There was somebody sitting in his old car.

6

"Can I come in?" Buddy asked, a few minutes later.

I stood aside. My son shouldered past me with his knapsack. Buck pushed a dinette chair in his direction.

I went to put on water.

"So your step-daddy found you," I said when we were sitting at the dinette table with three cups of my instant coffee, half milk and sugar. "How'd he know where to look?"

"I know where he was all along," Buck said. "Even after he left Madrid and Hardy."

"That old fool! He still driving that wagon all over the country, posing for tourists?"

"He took me in," Buddy said, and I thought of the inside of Hardy's wagon, packed to the ceiling with tin buckets and candlesticks, kerosene lamps and twists of rope, all more scenic than useful, smelling of dirty old man.

"After you kicked me out," Buddy went on, looking in his cup.

"You stole money out of my purse."

"There's worse around than old Hardy," Buck said. "He let the boy sleep in his wagon one bitter night nine years ago when he didn't have any place else to go."

"You told me it was either you or him," I said.

"Mad as a hornet." Buck smiled. "I didn't mean it the way you took it, Mel."

"I took it for real—scared I'd lose you."

"You wouldn't have lost me," Buck said with that look that lays me low, and I knew the walking rain was on its way.

I got up from the table. "Well, one thing for sure, we need to go food shopping. There isn't a thing to eat in the house."

"You mean you're planning to cook?" Buck asked, grinning.

I turned to my son. "What do you want to eat, Buddy?"

He shrugged, his mind gone someplace else. I knew his favorites: pork tenderloin with real mashed potatoes and gravy, iceberg salad, peach ice cream.

I picked up my purse, wondering where Buddy went when he looked that way. He always had been full of secrets.

Then I went out the screen door, and when I turned around to close it, I saw them—my two men—sitting at the dinette table, wrapped in a silence that looked comfortable as a raggedy old blanket.

What is it between men that feels solid and yet so soft, that has wetness in it? I had my broom—I was my broom, with her long hard spine. What would the rain do to me, when it came—wet my bristles? I didn't know, and not knowing was exciting.

I had to walk right past Buddy's car to get to my pickup.

I saw a girl in the front seat, wearing a pink dress, staring straight ahead to try to get out of seeing me.

I stopped by her rolled-up window. She should have been gasping in there like a fish—it was 110 in the sun, at least—but she looked cool, pretty blond hair all in place, lipstick fresh—a young woman who could have slid off the page of a magazine.

I knocked on her window. "I'm his mother," I said, loud enough for her to hear.

She rolled down her window with the sweetest smile. "I'm Bridget," she said.

She went on smiling, and I noticed her little white teeth, milk teeth, they looked like, and the prize-baby dimple in her chin; but I also noticed she wasn't that young, probably a few years older than Buddy. Gold earrings, I saw as she turned away, under the shelf of that beautiful blond hair.

"How come Buddy didn't bring you inside?" I asked.

"I guess he's waiting to spring the surprise," she said, pointing down at her lap with all ten fingers.

I leaned in the car window. She was pregnant, far along.

"His?" I asked.

"I wouldn't come all the way up here, carrying another man's child."

"Some might," I said, liking her spunk.

"He told me you'd be mad."

"I don't know what I am, as yet." Which was the truth; my head was spinning.

She nodded like that made sense to her.

"I'm headed for the supermarket. You go on inside, cool off."

"Oh no," she said, firm now. "I'll wait out here for Buddy."

Did he have her under his thumb, or what? I couldn't say; couldn't see my way clear at all, right then.

I headed on into town.

— 7 —

"Where'd you dig up that name?" I asked when they told me later they were thinking about calling the baby Sundance. We were sitting at the table, eating dinner.

"I like the way it sounds," Bridget said.

"What about your parents? They like that name?"

Buck shoveled a hunk of pork onto my plate. I reached over with my spoon and captured some onions.

"They don't care," Bridget said in a tone I already knew meant, Don't ask me any more questions.

"Bridget pretty much raised herself," Buddy told me, and I wondered if he'd taken on the task of being her interpreter. "We're alike in that."

Buck slapped more pork onto Buddy's plate.

"You two plan this baby?" I asked.

"Oh yes," Buddy said, a shade too fast.

"Why?"

Bridget took the lead. "I'm thirty-two," she told me, like that was all the explanation anyone would need.

"Time's a-wasting?"

"Something like that. I passed up the chance a couple of times," she added, looking down at her hands.

She hadn't touched her food.

I saw then what I wanted to see—some version anyway. A pretty girl, raised to show herself off like the lace on the hem of an old-fashioned petticoat. And to stay washed and ironed and covered up, too. Men had wanted her, from early on—Bridget knew that—and likely they had interfered with her school work and made her mother wild. But now she wanted her real life to start, and my son shining with all his problems looked like real life, for sure.

A baby. It changes everything. It changed me, for good. And I could see Bridget was wanting that, racing toward it—what life is. What it asks, what it takes.

Buck asked, "You two fixing on getting married?"

"Not right now," Bridget said. Buddy had already said, "No."

"You friends, or what?" I asked.

"Best friends," Bridget said.

"Well, I don't get it," I told them.

Buddy laughed. "Don't worry, Mom. I plan on sticking around."

"Your daddy didn't stick around," I told him.

"He wanted to," Buddy said.

I stared.

"You've looked up Paul."

"Actually, he's my stepfather," Bridget said.

"Good Lord in heaven!"

"There's plenty more pork here," Buck said.

"So you two are related!" And I saw it now.

"Not by blood," Buddy said, "but Dad did raise her. Hired me, as well, once I found him. I met Bridget when I was doing yard work for them."

"Alike as two peas!"

Bridget laughed. "We have our differences. But Paul—I always called him that, I was nine when he married my mother—Paul is like a father to us both."

"We're going to need all the help we can get," Buddy said quickly. "Dad and his new wife just took on a baby."

"My mother was number two. This one is number three," Bridget explained. "

"What about you?" I asked my son. "Your habit still taking everything you make?"

Buck jabbed me with his elbow.

"I'm clean, been through detox," Buddy said, and for the first time, I knew it was so. His eyes told me: flat, shallow, the eyes of a shadow that's lost what cast it.

"You'll be able to save now, Son," Buck said, like they'd talked it through already.

"Got to find a job, first." He slung his arm around Bridget and I saw he depended on her.

And then there was that likeness. You know how love melts people together? It was that, but more: Paul was working his magic, making opposite ends meet; and all of a sudden I remembered when I fed him the dry corn.

It was when I was well along with Buddy. We were barely getting by, and Paul took it into his head to start training with a shaman, an old Apache lady in Taos. I didn't set much store by such things; I wanted Paul to get a job. But I did go to the initiation, as they called it, and that old lady told me I could be "a human." All the rest of them were dressed up like animals. Paul was decked out in long johns dyed brown and a deer head, and I was supposed to feed him a handful of dry corn. I remembered now the way his lips felt on my palm and how he stared at me, chewing, and I felt like he'd somehow brought all this about, all these years later—the baby, and Bridget, and Buddy coming back to me.

"What do you want me to do?" I asked.

"Help us with the baby," Buddy said, prompt.

"I work," I told him, fast. "I have a life."

"You've got your evenings and weekends," Buddy said. "If we were living closer—"

"She dances," Buck told them. "Four or five nights a week."

"What kind of dancing?" Bridget asked, smiling at me.

"Just about every kind," I told her. "Salsa, Ballroom, Country."

"Well," Buddy said, smiling, too, "your little granddaughter may cut in on some of that."

"I don't think so," I said, and Buck tramped my foot, under the table. "I live to dance."

"Live to dance?" Bridget asked. "When you've been on your feet all day, waiting tables?" I knew then Buddy had told her something about my life.

"They're not the same feet," I said.

"Wait till you see her," my son said, like he was prophesying, and I remembered my first sight of him, twenty-nine years ago, staring up at the light in the delivery room ceiling like he'd already located the sun.

"She's going to fall out when she sees that baby," Buck was saying, patting my knee, and I wondered if that was what he'd been waiting for, all the years we were together.

I tried to put iron in my voice. "Listen, kids, I already put my time in," I said, "raising Buddy, alone, with next to no money. It almost killed me."

Buddy said, "Dad told me he looked for you everywhere."

"I never knew your dad to look for anything or anybody out of easy arm's reach," I told him, getting up to take the plates to the sink. "I lived a half a mile from him when you were two, used to catch a glimpse of him in town—"

"He thought you didn't want him." Buddy said.

"I didn't."

"Your mom's a tough nut," Buck said, and I was glad I had my back turned, washing dishes, because my face snarled up and I was close to crying.

Then they did what I least expected or wanted them to do—the two young people, Buddy and Bridget. They went out to their car and brought a package back, all wrapped up in pretty paper and tied with pink ribbons.

They made me open it right then, too, though it was getting late and I was dying to change my clothes.

Inside the wrapping paper there was a pink keepsake album with "Grandma's Pride and Joy" printed in calico letters on the cover.

I put my head down on the thing and bawled.

Buck patted my shoulder, and I could tell he was smiling at the kids, signaling them not to worry because a woman's true nature will have its way.

Bridget gave me her handkerchief—a real one, with a little rose at the corner.

"You don't have any idea—" I gasped, and that was as far as I got.

Now I watched Buck spoon me out a bowl of peach ice cream without telling him I'd long since lost my appetite.

They didn't notice for a minute that I'd left the kitchenette—they were talking—but then Buck came back to the bedroom. I was already halfway into my blacks.

"Not tonight," he said.

"It's Sunday," I reminded him. "Southwest is at the La Fonda."

"Not tonight," he said again.

I was putting on my eye shadow. "Don't try to stop me, Buck."

"It's not me, Mel, it's Buddy and Bridget. They need a chance to tell you more about what's happening."

"They can tell me tomorrow."

Buck was standing over me now, arms folded on his big flat belly. "This hadn't ought to be put off. First things first."

"First things first," I agreed, putting on my second coat of lipstick.

"You're acting dumb, Mel. There're some things you need to know."

I could see Buck and Buddy, going over those things one late night, down in El Paso.

"What's the all-fire rush?" I asked, standing up to slide my concho belt over my jeans. "You know what's going on, from the way you're acting. Isn't that enough, for now?"

He shook his head. "All right, then, here it is: Paul's married and settled down outside of El Paso—nice house, plenty of room."

"If he wants them . . ."

"He does. And you know Paul's no friend of yours. You're looking at losing your son and his baby."

I thought of the deer eating the hard corn. Paul would have his way. But not without me trying to get a little of what I wanted. "We'll see about that," I said.

Then I fluffed up my hair, perched my Stetson, tied my bandanna around my neck. "See you later."

"No, you won't," Buck said.

I stood there looking at him. Buck's not one to make idle threats. I cleared my throat. "You mean that, don't you?"

"Yes," he said.

"This can't be just Buddy. You never wanted to put up with him, before. Is it what I'm doing?"

Buck turned away, fiddled with stuff on the bureau. "I've tried to put up with it, Mel. I know you love it—"

"I do."

He said slowly, "It's turning you into somebody I don't know."

When I didn't say anything, he went on, "You used to tell me crack did that to Buddy—made him a different person, somebody you wouldn't even know how to speak to on the street. Well, it's the same thing, Mel. Dancing ought to be a controlled substance, too. They both have a pretty big effect."

"Maybe that somebody you don't want to know is the somebody I've always wanted to be."

"You sound like Buddy when he's high."

"You've got a good memory," I said.

"You weren't like this when I married you," he said, and I knew he meant he would never have married the woman standing in front of him now.

"How was I when you married me?" I asked. I figured from the quiet Buddy and Bridget were listening, so I raised my voice. "Tell me the truth, Buck."

He was embarrassed to say it, but he made himself. "You were soft, Mel, when it counted—"

I wanted to interrupt, "Where it counted?" My devil humor was coming up in a rush. I squashed it down.

"You cared," he went on. "You could cry. Tonight's the first time I've seen you cry in four or five years."

"Maybe I finally fixed my life so there isn't a lot to cry about."

He didn't say, what about the baby but I knew what he was thinking. "You got tough, Mel, and I don't like it."

"And you think it's my dancing." I was standing in the doorway now, the way he had, hands braced, and I knew I filled the space.

"It's the way you do it."

"Don't ten years count?" I asked. My voice was scratching my throat.

"Sure, they count," Buck said, flopping down on the bed, "but I thought sure Buddy—"

"I love Buddy. I don't love his problems, and I sure don't want to live with them," I said, making sure they could hear me, in the dinette. "I also love you, Buck. I don't want to lose either one of you," I said, my voice dry and cracking.

Then Buddy was in front of me, his hand on my shoulder. "You always used to want to be needed, Mom. Remember all those strays you picked up?"

"You were the one who brought them home—most of them. I love you, and your step-daddy, but I can't take care of either of you, now."

"We aren't asking for much," Buck said, and I thought again of the way they must have confabulated in some roadhouse south of here.

"I just need to stay off TV talk shows and quit dancing," I said, trying to smile. "The first one's easy. I've had my chance. The second one's just about impossible."

Now Bridget was in back of Buddy, looking over his shoulder. "It embarrasses them," she told me, like maybe I didn't already know. "You dancing with women."

"I like to lead. That's all there is to it. I like to lead a lot. Some people like green chili, I favor red."

Buck told me, "I'd dance with you myself—"

"No man worth his salt would let me lead."

They were quiet, then.

Then Buck told me what they'd all been waiting to say. "You aren't even that good. Women say you jerk them all around the floor."

"What women? Where'd you hear that?"

"They're saying it around town."

"I know some that'd say anything." I was flushing red.

I got through them somehow, all three packed tight in the door-way, and stomped out to my pickup. Yes, stomped: my boot heels quaked the particle-board floor. They'd found a way to shame me, finally; Bridget, bless her heart, had found it—and that was as good as dropping a noose over my head. I had to get out of there before they yanked it tight.

Driving down Cerrillos, I saw the mountains, bulking dark above the nest of town lights, and I knew I had to find a way to slip out of that noose.

8

I had to take dance lessons.

I knew that before I got to the La Fonda. Fight logic with logic, I thought, never my way before but the heaviest weapon I could lay my hands on. Besides, I was hurting, a raw place half-healed had opened up, and I knew I'd need to get salve from an expert.

I parked on the street outside the hotel and went to the payphone in the lobby. While I was thumbing through the busted-back telephone book, I heard the band, its heavy beat coming right down through the floor, and I knew they were going at it, up there.

I'll be up there again, I promised myself, once I can hold up my head with the best of them. Which can't be done with a hole in my confidence opened and oozing.

The downstairs bar within sight of the telephone was doing a brisk trade, and a couple of men were staring at me. They were trying to figure out whether I was fish, fowl, or good red herring; I didn't give them a clue when I tipped my Stetson, play-acting the dash and sass that used to come naturally. It occurred to me maybe I'd never have it again. Maybe I was going to lose Buck and Buddy, too, and it would finally break my heart.

I wasn't thinking about Buddy's baby, yet. That would come later. My list of loss was plenty long enough to start me shaking and feeling sick, inside.

Fight logic with logic, I thought. And it seemed to me, crazy as it sounds, that the men I loved might be proud of me, yet.

I was having trouble reading the listings in the Yellow Pages—my eyes were full of tears—but I finally figured out there was only one dance studio in town.

I put in my money and called.

A guy answered, and I could hear music and commotion behind him. He had one of those deep, from-another-world voices, all his words carrying downbeats in the wrong places: "Are you calling about our offer of two free lessons?"

"Yes," I said. It was as good a place to begin as any.

"Where'd you see our ad?"

"I didn't. I just want to improve my dancing."

"Which style?"

"All of them," I said.

"You've done some dancing?"

"A lot, but it seems I need to improve."

He began to rattle off details about time and place.

"I'd like to come in right now," I said. "It's urgent.

"Urgent?" He was tasting the word as though he appreciated its unusual flavor. "Okay. As it happens, I have a cancellation. How soon can you get here?"

I went out to my pickup, hopped in, and slammed a Bonnie tape into the deck. Right away she started wailing to the street lights, to the reflections in store windows, and I was heading out Cerrillos, back the way I'd come.

"Behind the ice cream place," he'd said, "the one with concrete benches outside."

Traffic was picking up, and I had trouble making my turn across the southbound lanes. Waiting, gripping the wheel, I felt my palms go wet and knew that would never do. You don't dance reeking and sweating. I relaxed my grip on the wheel, started to work on my breathing, remembering the yoga class I took one summer when Buck was still working and we could afford for me to indulge myself.

An opening appeared in the traffic the way it does when I stop waiting for it to happen, and I shot across.

There're a lot of little shopping centers off Cerrillos, prefab storefronts set in a row along a parking lot, not a tree in sight. This one had a dry cleaners and a couple of fast food places. Tucked between a Busy Burrito and an insurance office was a little storefront that advertised itself in all the colors of the rainbow: Desert Dancing.

I went in.

Light was fading outside, but inside was lit wall to wall with florescent, a white lake spreading to the mirrors. The mirrors reflected a handful of couples, dancing. Music and cold air blasted from an opening overhead.

Waiting for somebody to notice me, I took stock of a drove of dance shoes, scuffed and grubby, stuffed into an open cabinet.

Maybe it was the scuffed dance shoes—they looked familiar, like old work boots broken by honest toil. Whatever it was, I felt at home.

Then a man practicing the Rumba alone in the middle of the floor stopped what he was doing and came over: a tall guy with a full head of hair, dreadlocked like you don't see hair, even in Santa Fe, an Indian, and tall for one. He was wearing a black shirt and black jeans and dance shoes with heels that raised him well over six feet.

"I just telephoned," I said, introducing myself.

"My nine o'clock has the flu," he told me. "She canceled just before you called. You can have her time. Let me warm you up."

I nearly laughed. Nobody had offered to warm me up in quite a while.

Monty—his name—has a sure sense of rhythm; maybe he had a dancing bear for a great-grandmother, or some kind of cavorting guardian angel. Anyway, he could move. And he led me with his whole body, from the center, a firm center that made me feel safe.

Right away he swung me into the Rumba—he didn't ask me if I knew the step—and although the Rumba's not one of my best dances, I sank into his rhythm and followed him, letting him lead.

In the mirror I caught a glimpse of us dancing together, two beings nearly the same height and weight, both dressed in black. It wasn't clear who was teacher or pupil, man or woman, and I thought that was just what I wanted.

Monty whirled me to a stop. "Good," he said, with an enthusiasm I don't hear too much. "Sit down and tell me about your goals."

I thought he meant life goals.

We perched on the long bench that ran around the room.

"I only have one," I said, looking into blue eyes; he looked like he'd had a hard life, and come out of it on the right side. Handsome, but not smooth, not finished, as though life had begun working in him late but fast, like yeast. "I want you to improve the way I lead," I said.

"Why do you want to lead?

"I've been leading for years," I told him. "I'm no beginner. But some people—" I hedged a little—"don't seem satisfied with the way I do it." That wasn't quite the truth, but it was close enough. "And I want to take my lessons with a man."

I hadn't thought of that before, but it seemed obvious. A woman wouldn't have a strong enough frame (I learned later that's what you call it) to offer me the resistance I needed.

Resistance maybe isn't the word, but it's the best I can come up with, for now.

Monty looked at me "You didn't answer my question," he said.

"Let's just say other people have been leading me around by the nose my whole damn life-"

"Men?"

"Mostly. It's not their fault, it's what they're trained to do, but I need another way, now, and there is another way, I know that. I just need a little polishing."

"Well, I'll try it," Monty said. "When a woman knows what she wants—I kind of like it." Then he started to explain things to me. "A woman leading her partner is called back-leading. You can't let it show. All my lady teachers learn how to do it."

Good God, I thought. He's gone and agreed.

I sat there stunned while Monty went to get a clipboard with a list of prices for lessons, which you bought in a block. The prices were pretty substantial, and I was glad my checking account wasn't overdrawn, for once. I signed up for ten, then picked a six o'clock time slot so I could come straight from work.

Monty was still watching me, like I hadn't said enough.

"I like to see my partners get that glow," I said, looking at two women, who were practicing an underarm turn. "A good lead will do that, for a woman. I'm sure you've seen it."

"Many times," he said, and again I noticed his refined use of words, that seemed at odds with his face.

"All kinds of women, tall, short, young, old, plain, pretty—you can almost hear them sigh with relief when they settle into a strong lead. All their worries drop away. It can't be done in real life, but dancing's a harmless way of pretending."

He took that, too.

"Some people don't like me to do it," I said.

"Women?" he asked.

"Women and men."

He nodded. I wondered if he guessed I meant one man, in particular.

"I figure if I get really good at it . . . they might even be proud of me."

He nodded again. "You want to compete?"

"I hadn't thought about it, but I might." Buck might see me swirling under some spotlight, winning a big gaudy trophy.

The two women were passing us now in sweetheart position, looking like two pigeons perched on a limb.

"I love to move," I said, tapping my foot to the beat. It was time to dance and stop talking.

Monty stood up. "Let's try a Two-Step, Melody. This time you can lead."

"Everybody calls me Mel. I only sign receipts and checks with my whole name."

Then we started—and began one of the happiest times of my life.

For the first time in my entire life, I was holding a tall strong man in my arms, I was leading him from my center—as Monty called it—into the quick swirling patterns of the Two-Step. There was no skirt rustling against my knees, no sweet, salty smell of lipstick, sweat and perfume, but I had hold of a living body, blood, muscles, the whole deal, and this body bent to my will, even to my whim, not out of weakness but out of willingness, a kind of faith in motion.

I put him into what I call the Roundabout—it has another name, but I don't care for it. In the Roundabout, the partner being led runs forward, then circles around the partner who's stayed more or less in one place, and then they switch and he runs ahead and around her. It's a beautiful motion, like two butterflies circling each other, playing. Monty was so quick and light he hardly seemed to need the pressure of my hand and hip, and yet I knew his quickness and lightness were partly created by my firm, light lead.

At the end of the hour, I drifted out into the night with my receipt for ten lessons in my hand, ready, I thought, for whatever was coming next.

When I got back to the Wilderness, the lights were still on, although it was past ten. I wondered what was up.

Buck was sitting on our bed with his hands dropped between his knees, looking helpless and old. A hurricane had passed through the room; the lamp was knocked over, the picture of Yellowstone was hanging crooked, and our one chair was broken.

"What happened?" I asked, working to keep my calm.

"Police came and took him."

"Took Buddy?"

He nodded, looking finished. "There's a warrant out on him."

I sat down next to him. "Where's the girl?"

"She was screaming . . ." He sighed, shook his head. "Tried to throw the lamp at them. They handcuffed her too, took them both in the back of the patrol car."

"What're they charging him with?"

"Breaking parole, leaving Texas. And a new charge. The fool had something in his car."

"What?"

"Unregistered firearm, Smith and Wesson revolver, loaded."

I sat for a while without saying anything.

I'd been through so much with Buddy, and after a while it stopped sticking. I was scared and hurt and angry, but some part of my heart wasn't touched; that door closed a long time ago. Behind that door, the quick-step tape was still rolling, and Monty had his arm around me, showing me the turn-out.

Who would understand?

Did it matter, anymore, whether somebody understood?

I began for the first time in my life to think it didn't, and I knew then I wasn't going to let anyone, even my son, separate me from my happiness.

I turned into a dancer, then.

"He's in bad trouble back in Texas," Buck was telling me, and I put my arm around his slumped shoulders. "An old charge—prison, for possession and dealing, then parole; I don't know the details. Tony Manzano—the arresting officer—told me that much before they took them off. The girl was screaming it was all a set-up."

"I'm surprised Tony told you anything."

"His son's an electrician, he worked for me on a couple of jobs. Tony didn't say much, but he let me know it's serious. I don't think the girl knows anything except she's in love with him and she's going to have his baby."

"How'd Tony know they were here?"

"Fern," Buck said, and sighed. "Her telephone number was all they had down in El Paso." I wondered why my sister-in-law hadn't told me that. "When the probation officer called Fern—Buddy had no business leaving the state—she told him they'd left to come up here."

"Fern's a busy-body," I said.

"Fern doesn't lie for anybody, never has," Buck said. "Buddy must have known she wouldn't cover for him when he told her his plans."

That didn't make sense to me, but I didn't dispute it. "There isn't anything we can do now but try to get some sleep," I said, and I started to set the room to rights. My pretty pink glass lamp had a crack running clear through it; I put it in the closet. "Lucky we have the ceiling fixture—"

"Buddy yelled at me to tell you to come down and bail him out."

"I just spent all my money," I said. "My checking account's down to five dollars and sixty-one cents till next Friday."

"Mel, he's your son."

"I know that better than you do, but I stopped spending bail money on him years ago."

"What about the girl? She's pregnant," Buck said, as though I might have forgotten.

"She's in this up to her neck," I said. "There's no way I can pull her out. If she's going to stick with Buddy, she might as well get used to the inside of a jail."

Buck stood up. When he's annoyed, he swells to twice his size. "So you're just going to get undressed and go to bed—" I was taking my nightgown off the hook—"while those two kids—"

"You want them back, Buck, you go down and bail them out."

He glowered at me. "Your own flesh and blood—"

I stripped off my blacks and dropped my nightgown over my head. "Buddy's closer to me than flesh and blood. I love him more than anything in this world." I let that sink in. "But I learned the hard way to stay out of his messes."

Buck knew what I was talking about, only right then he didn't chose to remember.

"I told you what he did last time he was living with me." I was facing him, hands on my hips, and I remembered my mother standing that way, giving me a piece of her mind—an unwanted piece, usually. "Maybe he's done the same thing to Fern, and that's why she was so quick to turn him in. He tears up everything, Buck, when he's on the stuff. Phones ripped out of the wall, closets ransacked, dishes smashed. You can't live anymore in a place where he's been on the rampage."

"That was when he was using," Buck said. "You know what jail's like here?"

"No, and I don't need to," I said. "It's no better and no worse than the other places he's been. Buddy's smart, he'll have some jailhouse lawyer on the phone, making a ruckus about his rights."

"He's still going to have to spend the night there."

"You think that's the first night he's spent in jail? I know a lot about his rights," I went on, "but what about my rights, Buck? What about yours—ours? We worked hard for this place. Now I have to go out and buy another lamp, get that chair fixed."

He sat down again, looking whipped. I perched on the bed beside him. "I know this is tough," I said, patting his knee, "but this one time you need to follow my lead. I've been in Buddy's nightmare since he was thirteen years old. You saw the last little bit of it when we first got together, and I never wanted you to see any more. Now you have, but you still don't remember what it does to you. You still think love can fix him; I did too, for years. But this is more than love can fix, at least the kind you're thinking about, and we're both liable to go down the drain, trying."

"I know he has problems," Buck said. "But he's a good boy, under it all."

He looked at me then, and I lost my nerve. His look was cold as a pane of glass on a winter night, that dark, too.

"We probably won't be able to stay out of his mess for long anyway," I said. "He'll pull us into it, somehow. That's why he's back here, Buck. It's more than drugs, I know that now. It's some demon he has that won't let anybody rest. But at least we can get one more good night's sleep." I had a hunch it would be our last, for a long time.

Buck stood up then and unbuckled his belt. He took off his clothes like he was underwater, moving against a lot of weight. I climbed under the sheets and welcomed him in.

Falling asleep, I saw my picture of Yellowstone, hanging cockeyed on the wall; it's one of the places Buck and I always planned to visit, and I wondered if we'd ever get there, now.

Deep in the night, Buck asked me, "What'd you spend all your money on?"

"Dance lessons," I said.

9

Buddy got out of jail next day, I don't know how, white-hot mad at me for denying him bail, and Bridget was even madder.

They stood in my kitchen, wouldn't even sit down. I was worrying about being late to work, and there was Buddy with his arm around the girl, and I could tell they'd been working themselves up all the way out from town. "I don't know why I thought you'd help me," Buddy said. "You never have."

Buck was sitting hunched over the little TV like he couldn't hear a thing.

"I tried," I told Buddy, and then I turned around to fiddle with the percolator. I didn't want him to see the tears in my eyes.

"I've nearly starved, I've spend months in jail, Arizona, Texas—"

"For nothing," Bridget said. "Just plain nothing!"

I wondered when she'd decided to believe that.

Except deciding wasn't the right word. Buddy must have come over her like a storm.

"You won't even talk to me on the phone, most of the time," Buddy said.

"You call me at work. I'm sick of accepting charges." I poured myself a cup of coffee. "You're a grown man, how come you can't pay for your own calls?"

"I can't get a job," he told me. "You forget I'm a convicted felon, Ma? Nobody'll hire me, once they've check my record."

"Whose fault is that?" I asked, trying to taste the coffee. It was too hot, and bitter. "Who made you a felon?"

"The court system did!" Bridget shouted.

"Don't yell at me," I told her. "You planning to raise that baby outside the law?" I saw Buddy's shoulders slump like I'd leaned on them. "It's going to be a bastard, to start with. That's tough enough. No last name, and its Daddy on the run."

"It'll have my last name," Buddy said, like he'd just that minute decided. I saw Bridget look at him, grateful and surprised, and figured she hadn't dared to ask, for fear of hearing the wrong answer.

Buddy went on, "I don't expect to be on the run after it's born."

"You will be," I said, stringing myself tight as a barbed-wire fence; kindness never did anything for Buddy. I looked Bridget right in the eye and went on, "How're you going to take care of that child? You got any kind of medical insurance?" I hardly needed to see the head shake, the shrug. "Where's the money going to come from? I don't have any, and Buck doesn't either, and it sounds like Fern's washed her hands."

"She'll be sorry, I can tell you that much," Buddy said. "Maybe not right away, but down the road."

"I don't want to hear you threatening Fern, or anybody else," I said, that wire so tight now it twanged.

The girl shook herself together. "Let's get out of here, Buddy," she said, taking his hand. "We've got things to do."

They didn't even look back at me. They went out to his car hand in hand like a pair of teenage lovers.

Bridget still had on her little pink dress but it was torn and stained now. Still, she was walking like a queen and holding to my son—her shield and her scepter.

"God bless her," I said to Buck or the air or anybody who would listen. "Poor little thing, she doesn't anymore know what she's getting into . . ."

Behind me, Buck said, "Her family's got money, Mel."

That explained something about her, something I hadn't been able to figure.

"How do you know?" I asked, turning around; Buck was looking at me, the TV rattling away behind him.

"Fern called. She's done some checking with people she knows in El Paso, and it seems this girl's father's a bank president."

"So Fern hasn't washed her hands."

"I didn't say that. She's mad as a hornet—Buddy jumping probation. But she wanted us to know."

"Looks like Buddy's fallen on his feet again."

"That's how he got out of jail, I guess. The girl must have called her father."

"I'm going to be late for work," I said, heading for the door.

My first break, I called Fern from the phone at the cashier's desk. She had her Voice Mail on, and I left a good long message, thanking her for taking the hard road and turning Buddy in.

I guess I have learned something, all these years, I told myself. Don't take the easy way. Find a different definition for love.

But it was that girl, Bridget, with her pretty pink dress all stained and torn, and her big belly. I knew all about how stubborn she could be because I'd been that way myself, taking off with little Buddy, determined to make it on my own. I knew, now, the price we'd both paid, in something harder than money, and I didn't want Bridget and her baby to go through that. So Buddy had to be the one to take the hard way. He had to grow up.

I had my next dance lesson scheduled for six o'clock, right after my shift; I'd brought my shoes and a fresh pair of hose, and I changed in the bathroom before I left work. I noticed Mrs. Lopez watching me when I left, and I wondered if she was still holding my speaking up against me.

When I got to the studio, Monty told me he wanted me to learn the tango.

"Not the Argentine," I said. I'd seen enough of that on TV to know I wasn't ready for it.

"No, the American," he said, and then he looked at what I had on. "I know you have to come straight from work, but I can't see your knees in that long dress."

"I'll wear something shorter," I told him, and then I realized it was one of the few times in my life I've let a man tell me what to wear.

He took me into the Tango Basic without saying another word. I expected explanations, but that's not Monty's way. He wanted to feel if I could follow, before I started to lead, and I was soaking up the way he moved me, not with his arms, but with his chest, stomach, thighs—the contact so light I hardly felt it.

"I always thought you had to use pressure, to lead," I told him, watching myself in the mirror.

Then he showed me the Side-Step, and I saw how neatly his small, soft-looking, scuffed black dancing shoes pivoted on the floor. He showed me a head turn, that was like that flick Birds of Paradise make when you come up to their fence in the zoo: fierce. I wasn't to do that yet, though. That was advanced.

He adjusted my stance with both hands, saying, "Stomach in, shoulders relaxed, weight forward on the balls of your feet," and I wondered why I who was always flicking off my customers' hands could accept his so easily. I was pure possibility to Monty, a body that might learn to dance, and I hadn't been that to anyone, even when I was a child.

"I wish life was more like this," I blurted out when he dipped me into what I learned later was a Corté.

Monty didn't say anything. I guessed he was used to hearing women say they wished life was more like dancing, probably women, like me, who won't let men open car doors for them.

All this time, the mournful tango music was circling around me, and when Monty led me again into the Basic, the music seemed to wing my feet, and I thought suddenly of those folding chairs outside the Wilderness, flying away across the desert.

Did they matter, now? Did anything matter, except the way I was moving?

At the end of the tango, Monty went back to his glory-hole, leading me by the tips of my fingers. Along the way, he introduced me to a pretty young woman wearing a short red dress that flared out like the cup of a tulip. "This is Caroline," Monty told me, and I knew she must be something special.

Monty put on another Tango, and this time we did the basic steps in silence. I didn't need words anymore—instruction—not because I understood what Monty was teaching me—I didn't, maybe never would—but because another language was operating.

— ~ —

"I want to learn what you do," I told Monty, at the start of my third lesson.

He didn't say anything. He was sitting on the bench beside me in his at-ease position, hands clasped and dropped between his knees, feet a little turned out in his small scuffed shoes. Already I'd noticed the only time he sat down was between one lesson and the next—one or two minutes while a woman was leaning over to fasten her shoe straps.

(Years later, I'd wonder how he stood the contact with all of us, the smells, the feel, but I was too new then to Monty's world to think of the way it might affect him, that physical closeness with a bunch of strangers.)

"Can you do that?" I asked, straightening up—I'd asked the question with my head between my knees, strapping my shoes.

"Yes," he said, and I noticed for the first time how pale and tired he looked.

Then he stood up, hands on hips, facing me. "We have two women taking lessons who dance together. One leads for a while, then the other does."

"I saw them, but I don't have a woman to practice with," I told him. "Don't plan to, either. A straight woman would freak if I asked her to dance with me in broad daylight, and I don't care for the other kind."

"We try to teach what people want to learn," he said, and I thought of car payments and rent due. He wasn't free to refuse.

I wanted to apologize for getting what I wanted, but I was already leading him into the first slow, long movements of the Two-Step, and I could feel him coming along with me, his fine dancer's body trained to respond to signals no matter who was giving them, and the happiness I felt on the dance floor at Club Alegria when a stranger floated into my arms began to beat against me again like strong surf, carrying everything in front of it, and I didn't care, anymore, what Monty thought or felt—

because we were sailing across that wide smooth floor, and he was responding to me, counting the beat but still responding to me— slow, slow, quick, quick, the prettiest pattern of all the dances, gaining momentum till we were whirling around the room.

Then he stopped me, stopped the music, and began to show me, in the mirror, how to adjust my frame, how to place my hands, and then he started to work on my leg extension, and on the placement of my feet, and I knew I had a lot to learn, and that he was going to teach me.

We did a lot of practice steps, side by side, watching in the mirror,

Monty correcting me, and all the air went out of it, and I started to hear the telephone ringing at the desk, and Caroline taking messages, and to notice other people coming in for their lessons, carrying their dance shoes in little bags, and the instructors going to the door to greet them.

Then my hour was almost up—I'd started to notice the big clock on the wall by the door to the bathroom—the ninety-five dollars I couldn't afford and that should have gone to my son's bail almost gone, and Monty went to his glory-hole and put on another CD, and it was Bonnie.

She was wailing about growing old, facing those lines in the mirror, giving up on love and then finding it in the nick of time.

Monty stood with his arms up, one knee bent, poised and ready to go, and when I settled my arm around him and took hold of his hand—a little damp now, a little warm, from all that contact—I thought of a woman playing a cello I'd seen once on TV, spreading her knees in a long skirt, clasping that big wood cello between her thighs, and I knew it didn't have to be that obvious—leading—to be the most important thing in the world.

"Scared of running out of time," Bonnie was singing in her sweet, rough, know-all voice, and I drew Monty into the Two-Step the way I draw my shadow along behind me when I'm hurrying out of the parking lot at Rita's on a hot day, and for a minute it all came together: Buddy, and Buck, and Bridget, and the baby—my grandchild—and my parents' graves, back in the Purchase, and my own, unknown grave, already waiting somewhere in the desert, and I counted with Monty, "Slow, slow, quick, quick," knowing there wasn't a chance, now, that we'd ever lose the beat.

10

Next morning I hopped in my pickup, slid a tape into the slot, turned on the motor and pumped up the AC. I'd already cried a bucket: at two AM when I somehow knew Buck wasn't coming home, and at six, the sun rising in a cloud bank, when I finally found his note on top of the TV, and later at work when Buddy called collect with Bridget just behind him in the payphone booth and said they were on the lam, heading south.

I told Mrs. Lopez it was a family emergency. It was. But what cut into me was being alone again, as though the years with first my son and then my husband had hardly existed, as though aloneness was my true and inescapable fate.

I turned on Rodeo Road and hit the throughway heading south. Bonnie was singing "Love Letter," and I wondered if there was a way of looking at Buck's note as a love letter; it seemed to me he'd left room for that. "I'll be gone for a while. Take care of yourself"—scrawled on the back of a grocery store receipt. And then the little cross he makes that signifies a kiss.

It left room for hope.

Ten days ago when I hit the throughway going south, I was heading for New York; just a little while back, but already that trip seemed as unlikely as a flight to the moon.

This time, I thought, I'll run away on the ground, or leastwise on the cement.

I turned off at Algodones and headed west, out where the big table-top mesas march away from the banks of the Rio Grande.

There was a lot of truck traffic heading west, straight out across the plains, and a long freight threading its way through dusty sage: high summer, and everybody and everything moving. It was a relief to turn off the main drag and head north into the Jemez Mountains. Fields of corn along the road showed leaves tall and glittering, and the little old Spanish towns didn't seem to have a soul left in them. Everybody had gone up to the feast day at Jemez Pueblo.

I love the dances.

I used to try to get Doris or Buck to go with me, but Doris doesn't like standing in the sun—and Buck doesn't see the point. For a while there I thought I wouldn't want to go into foreign territory alone. Now, I know better.

Those dances show me something: how life can be lived to a drum beat, how dancing can move you into a clear space of light.

There's no leading in the Indian dances, and no following, except in the long line where the dancers turn around slowly, one after the other. That gave me something to chew on.

The entrance to the pueblo was just about blocked with parked cars, herded around the police station and the Head Start building. I took a right onto a dirt road and parked in the shade of a big cottonwood. Tumble-down sheds and a cage of chickens reminded me I was parking on somebody's home territory, but I decided to take the risk.

Locking the truck, Buddy's voice came back to me: "We're going down to El Paso to see Dad."

Since when did you call Paul Dad? I wanted to ask. Since when did you even have an address for your father—who never sent a check or a present or came to see you the whole time I was raising you? But it was too late for all those questions. They were already halfway to the big house outside El Paso, the wife and husband waiting at the door.

I thought I knew what that meant: I might never see them again, or only rarely.

I walked up to the pueblo, enjoying the look of their houses: low, flat adobes with bald dooryards. A giant cornstalk was sprouting in one of those yards, looking pampered as a household pet, and there was a crowd of children hanging out on the porch. Nobody else in sight, except for some tourists like me, trying to figure out which way to the plaza, and some Indians selling pricey drinks and trinkets.

Then I heard the drums, far off, on the other side of the houses. All of us turned around and headed toward that sound. The drums have a way of calling you, no matter who you are. That beat doesn't make distinctions. And I thought of the Man saying after one of his parables, Those who have ears to hear . . .

The drums lead you in the direction of salvation, like the tango music, my last lesson. Away from words and their little catches, toward the heart and the soul.

I threaded my way through slits between houses and found myself on the edge of a big open plaza.

There must have been close to two hundred people dancing, men and women in two long lines that stretched from one end of the plaza to the other: the men's bare chests were painted red, crossed by bandoleers of cowrie shells, and they wore white embroidered kilts, beaded belts, animal skins with the tails hanging down behind.

Their women were decked out, too, with jigsaw turquoise-painted wooden headdresses, feathers, and long black skirts. Some of them were barefoot, stepping fast on the hot sand.

At the head of the two lines, thirty or forty elders were singing and beating their drums.

Then I saw the bull, prancing down the line of dancers. He wore a splotched black-and-white hide with a dangling tail, and the cow bell around his neck jangled as he trotted. Every time he passed a knot of men, the bull would stop and sway his horns, and I caught sight of the hole under the head where the dancer draws in air and looks out. The edge of the hole was rimmed with pinned-on dollar bills. Now and then an Indian would step forward and pin on another bill, and the bull would prance and nod his thanks.

I guessed what they were paying for, and praying for: luck, rain, a good harvest, many sons.

I needed luck, if not the rest.

I stepped forward with a dollar bill in my hand. The bull turned away, but I wasn't going to put up with that. I went along with him down the line of dancers, and pretty soon—hoping to get rid of me—he turned around and made a pass at me with his horns. I caught sight of the man's face inside the opening, and he wasn't smiling.

I stepped fast to one side to avoid the horns, which were real, and reached in at the same time and pinned my bill alongside the others.

The bull careened away, without his usual courtesy.

I didn't care. I'd done what I meant to do.

Good luck, or bad luck—either way, I thought, something new will happen. It was out of my hands.

The bull was not the dancers, though, and I went back to watching their simple steps, pounding the earth. Those steps were hard rain, and hope, and the turning in place was the seed drilled into the dirt. I thought of the dirt under Monty's dance floor, how dark it must be, and moist, how it was once a cornfield sending shoots up to the light.

Our steps carry us there. The dancers' steps on the dirt plaza, and mine on the wooden floor: a little closer to where we need to be.

They stopped for a break, and I went to buy myself something to eat. Outside the plaza, a tribal policeman, looking fierce in his belted uniform, was taking the film out of a camera some Anglo had brought, walking right past the big green sign that says No Cameras, No Note-taking, No Sketches.

A bunch of Navajos was cooking up sheep stew and fry bread in a shed. I ordered myself a piece of fry bread and watched the woman behind the counter roll out a circle of dough and drop it into popping hot oil. The circle came out puffy and golden, and I drenched it with honey from her sticky plastic bottle.

Then I went back to my pickup, parked under the cottonwood.

Before I climbed in, I realized I had to pee something terrible, and after a careful look around, I unzipped my jeans and squatted down behind my front tire.

I was just about done when I heard something. There was nothing for it but to finish, looking down at the pool spreading between my boots.

Then I pulled up my pants and turned around. An Indian man was standing right behind me.

"My land," he said. His eyes were flat as pennies.

"Sorry," I muttered; my pee was already disappearing into the dust. "No harm done, or intended."

"My land," he said again, stepping toward me.

I jumped in the truck and locked the door.

Peeling out of there, I started to laugh. And I thought, Am I losing it? Is this why Buck vamoosed? Is this why Buddy's mad at me? Because I do things like pinning a dollar bill where I have no business pinning it and peeing on some guy's land?

It seemed likely.

It also seemed likely these were two things I needed to confess to Father Garcia.

I drove away, thinking how often I'd had these moods, done these things: sleeping with men I had no business sleeping with, taking off at odd hours for unknown destinations, leaving smoking ruins behind.

I drove fast back to Santa Fe and the little adobe church by the acequia.

"I'm taking San Juan Nepumuceno for my patron, from here on out," I told Father Garcia at the end of my confession.

He corrected the way I said the saint's name, his voice filtered through the carved wooden screen, "At this point you want the help of the patron saint of secrets?"

I nodded. The good father had wrapped me for half an hour in his listening, firm and warm and close as a pair of human arms. "I've told enough secrets for this lifetime," I explained. "At least that's the way I see it now. If I never had tried to talk to Buck about my dancing . . ."

"Maybe you chose the wrong people to receive them."

"That's all the people I know, it turns out. Fern doesn't get it, Doris doesn't even want to hear, my son and his girlfriend are too mad at me to hear anything I say—but still, I try, more fool me." I thought of the old *mea culpa*, fist to breast; it seemed to go with what I was saying.

Father Garcia said, "Remember, Melanie, you insisted on going dancing that evening when Buck asked you to stay home."

I made a fist in the darkness and lightly tapped my breast. "You're right. I did." I drew a breath. "And I believe I'd do it again, too, even if I knew for sure Buck was going to leave. Is that the sin of selfishness, Father?" I'd already been absolved of several kinds of sin, but now they all seemed to add up to the same thing. "Maybe it wasn't the dancing made him leave, anyway. How do I know? And even if it was . . . You must pay a price for playing music every Friday—"

"You had an obligation to put your marriage first," Father Garcia interrupted. "Remember your vows."

"I didn't say any vows. A justice married us."

"You must have thought them."

He knew me too well.

"Maybe, but thinking is not the same as saying. We chose the justice, it wasn't an accident."

"And no children. In my experience, a marriage not blessed with children . . ."

"We had Buddy," I said, and laughed. "We may even have him still."

Father Garcia was silent, and I wondered if I'd shocked him, at last. But he's heard that before—the laugh of the breakdown, the tearing sound that comes when you let it all go.

He began to give me his blessing.

Tears came, fast, after that. I leaned my forehead on the little shelf under the grill and sobbed.

Stepping out from behind the curtain, I wiped my face on my sleeve.

Then I walked out of the big dark church into the desert afternoon, and shrugged as though I was throwing off a heavy winter coat. A part of the day was still left, for me alone. It almost never happened. Days-off and holidays were taken up ordinarily with catching up on cleaning and errands, doing the laundry, maybe going somewhere with Buck for a beer, but a day to myself, even a piece of it, was something different.

When I got home, there was a commotion going on next door. A minute later the owner, Bill, was hammering on the door and, then two people came flying out like bees from a hive. They took off in their old Chevy and Bill, coming behind them, locked the place up and put the key in his pocket.

I was out the door before I had time to think.

"It's not right," I said into Bill's homely face.

"They're making a commotion, there've been complaints."

"We got some rights here," I told him. "You throw them out, I might be next."

"Never had a spot of trouble—"

"Till now. What if I raise my voice some night you're in this mood? Run the TV too loud, too late? What if when you come sneaking around to check on me, I lock the door on you and tell you to get the hell away?"

Old Mr. McPhee down the road had come out to see what was going on, and the woman on the far side of the Wilderness was standing in her door.

"I always have liked Buck," Bill said, like it would calm me down.

"Me, too," I told him. "But I don't know if I'm ever going to see the bastard again."

And then all three of them were crowded around me, clucking and patting.

11

They may have thought they quieted me down, but I spent the night chewing on a hard lump of anger—aren't we all in this together?-, and in the morning I went over to the couple's trailer. I'd heard their car creep by at 2 AM—reduced to sneaking into their own place, to get past Bill.

At the door, I stopped for a minute to listen. It was quiet as death.

I knocked.

The girl came. I saw her through the glass pane in the door. She had on a man's shirt and nothing else, as far as I could tell. Her feet were bare, and her toenails were painted bright pink.

She cracked the door. "Come on in."

I did. She went back to the bedroom. I looked around. The place was a wreck. Not much to begin with, and that little bit thrown high, wide and handsome. Broken dishes on the floor, ceiling fixture pulled down, glass everywhere. The pitiful little curtains over the sink were wrenched off their rod, and it was bent double. By the door they'd hung one of those framed prayers: "Bless Our Home." Somehow that hadn't gotten hurt. I wondered how she could stand looking at it.

She came back, zipping her jeans.

"Somebody in a bad mood?" I asked, nodding toward the bedroom.

"PMS. You know."

I guess she saw me do a double-take.

"He always gets mad when it's my time of the month. My mom was the same way. Drove my dad wild, regular as clockwork, nagging for angel food cake. He was Navajo, we grew up on the rez, you had to drive fifty miles to buy a box of cake mix."

"You don't look Indian," I said. She was blond, thin and wiry as a pipe stem cleaner.

"He wasn't really my dad. We called him that, trying to stay out of his way. Not that it did us much good. He chased us around the house with the broom, when he felt like it. Never caught me, though. I don't know what he would've done if he had." Then she drew up short. "I'm Jean," she said, sticking out her hand.

I shook. "How come your husband—"

"He's not my husband. We're common-law by this time, I guess. Seven years."

"When did all this start?" I stepped, and glass crackled under my feet.

She picked up the curtains and started to string them back on the bent rod. "We do all right, most of the time. He always says he's sorry."

I backed up. "My name's Melanie. Pleased to meet you." I stuck out my hand, but she didn't take it. "I hear you're getting your asses thrown out of here. Bill's fed up."

She went on stringing. "That asshole."

"He's no favorite of mine, but he owns this place."

"There're other places."

"You thought about what it's going to cost you to move?"

She shrugged. All at once she'd gone limp as a slice of white bread soaked in water.

"Even if you could afford it, it still wouldn't be right," I told her. "Some places, you'd have recourse, you'd have something written in your lease, to protect you." I was heating up now. "Not here. Not required in the blessed state of New Mexico, far as I know. What's a complaint? A year ago, we put up with Bill's son shooting out the light on the corner every time he tied one on. Did anybody say anything? No . . . . But that was Bill's son. He's got protection. The same thing you need."

The line of her shoulders straightened. "I remember that boy shooting out the light." She laid the curtain down. "I said to Marty, 'How come you don't do something about it?'"

That's when I decided. There was something I could do here, something that would help. It felt like taking the first step out of quicksand.

"I'm going door to door, telling people what's happening," I said.

"Wait a minute—"

"You want to let Bill put you out, go right ahead. You must like taking the blame. You already got Marty believing it's your PMS makes him trash the place. Go right on the same way, if you want to. But I'm warning the neighbors what they can expect if they get on somebody's nerves. We're all on the same piece of thin ice."

I was already out the door by the time she made up her mind.

"I'll come with you," she called after me. "Wait up!"

"To make sure I don't say too much about what went on in there?"

She came out the door smiling. I didn't know till then she had a smile. "Maybe. But I also want to be in on it—whatever you're going to start. Marty's all the time nagging me I don't do anything but sit around."

"You want to leave him a note?"

"Nothing to write on."

I dug an old gas receipt out of my pocket. She had a pencil. She pushed the receipt up against the wall and printed on it in big black letters:

GONE ORGANIZING

Then she pushed the note between the screen and the door. "That's a pretty fancy word," I told her.

"You got a better one?"

I shook my head.

"The only thing pulled Daddy out of drink was all that carrying on about getting our land back. Mom said he found his dignity, going around the rez with petitions."

"You going to find your dignity, too?"

She turned that thin blond face toward me, pale as the sickle moon. "I already found it," she said, "once or twice, but it seems like I misplaced it somewhere."

I laughed. "You ever been dancing?"

"Way back," she said, "before—" and I saw that shine in her eyes.

"You want to take a step off Planet Earth, that's the way to do it," and right there in the dirt and litter I showed her the basic Rhumba step. "I'll teach you sometime."

"Alright!"

"But first," I told her, "we've got to get you out of your pickle."

And so we started.

12

Bill was sitting in his Chevy next morning when I went by on my way to the boxes to get the mail.

"Come here a minute," he called.

It was the day after Jean and I started the petition, and I'd been waiting for him to get his two cents in.

"Morning, Bill," I said. He was sitting like a big cabbage on his busted front seat, and he had his whole life spread out next to him: cigarettes, lighter, beer, an open bag of chips, a greasy wrench, some other tools, an old newspaper turned to the funnies, and work gloves shaped to the hands that wore them, lying curled together like pups.

"They fire you over at Rita's?" he asked.

"I'm on at noon today," I told him, not rising to the bait. If I had, I'd have told him I've never been fired from a job the entire thirty-two years I've been working, a point of pride I didn't much want to blunt on old Bill.

"Time to kill," he said, like he was talking to Buck about me. "Going around stirring up trouble, nothing better to do." Bill came out here from Tennessee a long time ago, but he'll never lose that mountain twang or that mean way of talking to a woman like it was behind her back.

"I guess you mean our petition," I said. There was a copy nailed to just about every spindly piñon in the park.

"Those there are my trees, you know that, Mel? You ain't got no business nailing something on them. Like to kill them, then where're you be for shade come next summer?" When I didn't give him the satisfaction of an answer, he saw fit to remind me, "Every square foot of dirt in this place belongs to me."

"That's so, but we lease it from you for good money. We got some rights, same as anybody who rents an apartment from a regular landlord." I didn't know if that was so but the way I saw it, it ought to be.

"You got the right to act decent," he came right back at me. "I never had no trouble with you and Buck, till now—"

"Eight years."

He nodded. "One of the first to move in. That's why I'm giving you another chance. 'Sides, I kind of like old Buck." He pushed a cigarette up out of his pack, stuck it in the side of his mouth and flicked that lighter eight or ten times before it fired. "He run out on you again?"

"What do you care, as long as the rent's paid regular?"

"Better be," he said. "I don't make no special deals-" and he winked, the old snake.

"Jean and Marty pay regular."

"That's so, but they cause too much commotion."

"You still think you're going to run them out?" I leaned in the window and he blew a stream of smoke right in my face.

"You damned right I'm going to. I told them already. Forty-eight hours to get their shit together, and that's more than I ought to give them."

"All we're asking for is a square deal," I told him, seeing I had him down for the count. "You read our petition, didn't you?"

He shrugged. I knew he'd probably been out at midnight with a flashlight, reading it on some tree when he hoped nobody would see him.

"I've got a copy right here for you." I pulled it out of my back pocket and uncreased it. "We've got twenty-seven signatures already—nearly half your people."

He glanced at it, then handed it back. "I don't need this aggravation, Mel."

"I know you don't." I wasn't having any trouble seeing his side of the picture; I knew he was going to mention his ulcers, next. "All we want from you is some words in our leases so we have warning before you throw us out, and a month to find another place if you do evict us."

"Who's this us?" he asked. "You and Buck?"

He had me there. I didn't say a thing.

"You been talking to a lawyer," he went on, seeing he had me cornered. "Well, I got a lawyer, too. Give me that thing back, I'll take it on down to him."

"I haven't been to see a lawyer, Bill, and I don't plan to. I don't aim to pay an arm and a leg to prove something that's just plain good common sense." I started going over the paper, my pointer finger under each word. "Twenty days grace period after the first warning—"

"The first warning! How many times you expect me—"

I rode right on. "A council made up of residents and the owner or his representative to review the complaint. Thirty days warning of any eviction process."

"My old timers are never going to sign that thing, Mel. They ain't looking for trouble."

"I thought Buck and me were your old-timers."

"I mean Chuck and Mary back there by the fence. They been here since before you guys."

That old couple must have leased the first lot Bill offered, within sight and sound of the throughway. For backyard they have his boundary fence, festooned with litter.

"We've already been by them," I said. "They took some persuading, but they signed. Look, here's their names. And below them, Minnie and David Stokes. Mr. Ortiz, too." I pointed out his crabbed signature; Raymond Ortiz hadn't been able to find his glasses when we went by, and so Jean printed his name underneath his signature. "We're going around this evening to talk to the ones that asked us to come back."

He was studying the list. "Evelyn Ortega's not on here."

"Just because that poor widow's soft on you . . ."

He came as close to blushing as he knew how to do.

"Okay," I told him, "saying we can't get Evelyn and a few other 'fraidy cats to sign. They'll be the only hold-outs. Mighty lonely position to be in. What's the widow going to want in return, Bill?"

He knew what I meant. Some girl from up in Colorado lived rent free for six months after she fixed things with Bill; we used to see him coming out of her beat-up Land Cruiser every Sunday morning at nine AM, like clockwork. Buck even teased him about getting up in time for church.

Bill drove off with the petition on the seat beside him, on his way to the statehouse, I guessed, where he has cronies, every one of them a lawyer.

I went on down to get the mail.

Then I showered and dressed for work; it was getting onto eleven, and I had errands to do in town.

I'd been doing pretty well on tips, the last few days—enough to pay the taxes on my take-home pay. It was Indian Market time, and while we don't get the big collectors eating at Rita's, we do get Mr. and Mrs. Ordinary Tourist with a hundred bucks to throw away on a little black pot made at one of the pueblos up the road, and a hankering for what they think is authentic New Mexico food, which at Rita's is pretty much just Tex-Mex with extra helpings of Christmas chile.

My rule is and always has been I keep my tips myself, no accounting to Buck given or asked for, while my paycheck goes straight into our joint checking account. I'm pretty sure Buck knows I make more in tips in a good week than I do in straight pay, but then I never ask how much of his retirement money he squirrels away in his savings account or gets rid of some other way. Even married people deserve some privacy.

After the ruckus started over what I was spending on dance lessons, I began saving my tips in my top drawer instead of spending the money right away on this and that. Before I left for work, I went in that drawer and counted.

So far, I had a hundred and forty-seven dollars plus some change, which meant I could finally get boots to wear to the Country-Western Fiesta in Albuquerque, coming up in about two weeks. You can't wear regular cowboy boots to dance because they're stiff-soled and heavy and make that clunking noise when you step out.

There's an outfit at De Vargas Mall that sells Country-Western stuff, and I went down there right after work to see what they had in the way of boots. It's a big barn of a place with too much in it, so it took me a while, wandering those long aisles piled high with boxes, to find what I wanted. I had the boots I was looking for pretty clearly in mind. They were going to be red, calf-high, with some tooling.

The pair I found was red, with a vine motif, twins to the ones I had in mind.

As soon as I sat down to try them on, one of those sales girls who wait to see if you're serious came to ask could she help.

I asked her to get me a pair of cotton socks; dancing, your feet sweat a lot, and the cotton absorbs it. She came back fast and cheery with the socks in her hand.

"You going to the Fiesta in Albuquerque?" she asked while I was dipping my left toes into a boot.

"Counting on it."

"Which routines?"

"Country Waltz and Two-Step, maybe Cha-Cha."

"You got your outfits?"

"Calf-length denim skirt for the Country Waltz and the Two-Step. I might get something a little shorter, for the Cha-Cha."

"Not too short, they measure your skirt with a yardstick before they let you on the floor."

"I heard that. It's supposed to be a family type thing. They wouldn't want to know what goes on in most families."

She went off to see might they have some kind of dress for the Cha-Cha; I told her I didn't want to spend more than fifty dollars.

Meanwhile I was still trying to wedge my left foot down in that boot.

"It's too tight," I told her when she came back with a dress over her arm.

"They're meant to fit snug." She put the dress down, then leaned over and started to tug on the boot. It wouldn't move. She suggested a plastic bag. "I can't dance in plastic," I told her, but she swore I wouldn't need it after the first time.

The plastic worked. My foot inched on down. I looked up and caught the eye of a tall man standing over near the mountain of boot boxes.

Real tall. That was all I registered. Six foot four, or maybe even five.

Right then I wondered what it'd be like to lead him. The women I'd been dancing with were all my height or shorter.

"You going to Albuquerque?" I asked, standing up to test my boot.

"I'm going to watch," he said. "I'm not good enough yet to take part."

I liked the way he talked, that crisp old-fashioned way of choosing his words carefully and placing them exactly in order.

Blue eyes crisped at the corners and a kindly, homely face with the same long jaw you see in horses leaning over the top rail of a fence. No ring—I looked right off. Neat pressed cotton shirt, a leafy kind of green, and pants tight enough to show a high butt and long legs. Brown boots, plain and well-used, not fancy. No flash, but something solid.

"You got a partner?" I asked him.

"I told you, I'm not good enough yet." It didn't seem to bother him.

That girl was standing there gawking like men and women never met at the Western Warehouse.

"You willing to learn?" I asked him. Strike while the iron is hot, I always say.

He didn't answer. He was staring, too.

"I'll give you till I get the other boot on," I told him, starting to wedge my right foot down into it. It was a two-person job, getting that boot on without the plastic bag, and I wondered out loud how I was going to manage it, alone.

"I don't promise to pull on your boots," the tall man said in that careful way, "but if you're willing to help me learn how to Two-Step . . ."

"I'll have to lead," I said. "There isn't any other way to teach you. I'm good, I'll teach you fast." To prove it, I did the basic step, sliding across the bare floor: slow, slow, quick, quick, and then a traveling turn.

"Let me show you," I said, holding up my arms. He was new enough to take the woman's position without even knowing what it was, just following a light pressure of my hands and arms.

I braced my frame the way Monty taught me and leaned into him. The first pressure, and he responded like a good car taking a slow banked turn. He didn't know what he was doing, but he was following. Big and tall as he was, he moved light on his feet. I looked down and saw my red boots gleam.

There was a narrow space between the piles of boxes, room enough for the basic step and a traveling turn, that's all. I couldn't show him the Sweetheart or the Rope Twist or any of the other fancy steps I'd been working on for weeks.

"Later I'll show you some more," I promised, then turned him out under my arm. It was a little awkward—I had to reach up high, to clear his head.

When we finished, that fool girl started clapping.

"What's your name?" I asked him.

"Arthur," he said, like his last name was a secret. I didn't need it, anyway. I wasn't going to be looking him up in the phone book.

"I'm Mel," I told him, and reached out to shake his big warm hand. "We'll have to practice, to get ready for Fiesta. We can dance the amateur routines in Albuquerque, and the Jack and Jill, after I get finished with the Pro-Am. What time's good for you to meet me at the dance studio? We need that floor, and the mirrors."

He looked all of a sudden like he was going to back out—before we even got started.

"This is just about dancing," I told him. "I'm a married woman, I'm not looking for trouble. But if you give me a chance, I'll teach you everything I know, for free, and you can take it from there."

"Sounds like a pretty good deal," the girl said, behind me.

That almost spoiled it.

"What will it do for you?" he asked, still uncomfortable.

"Give me a chance to dance with a tall man." I said it without flirting, knowing he didn't need or want extra sugar.

"I get off work at five," he said, "and it takes me about forty-five minutes to drive down to town from the Labs." By the Labs he meant Los Alamos, the poison factory up on the hill. I found out later he was a security guard, good pay, responsibilities.

He went on off then, and I grabbed that dress off the girl's arm and took it back to the trying-on booths.

It was red—my favorite color, these past few years. A flared skirt, and some kind of sparkle in the material.

I slipped it on, and looked to see whether too much leg was showing. I wasn't sure—the dress was pretty short—so I went out to find the girl.

She was waiting for me, eyes just full of stars.

"You think they'll let me on the floor in this?"

She went for a yardstick, and of course they didn't have one. Yardstick, the word and the thing itself, went out a long time ago. So she said she was sure the judges would pass on the dress, family event or not. She was just too happy with what she thought she'd seen—the start of something she thought was going to be more than a dance.

Well, fools can dream.

I studied myself in the long mirror, and then I saw the tall man behind me, reflected in the glass.

I turned around. "What do you think?" I asked, hands on my hips. "Will this be right for the Cha-Cha?"

"I don't know a thing about the Cha-Cha, but that dress looks fine."

I turned back to the mirror. "I'll never be a girl again—I hardly was when I was the right age—and this dress was made for somebody about sixteen."

"Age ain't nothing but a number," the girl said.

"I'll have to look some more," I told them both.

"It looks pretty on you, Mel," Arthur said.

"It's too short." Then I did a turn, and the skirt flared. My thighs were flashing, and I was glad I'd worn my one pair of sheers. I have nice legs—the compliment Buck usually pays me when I'm dressed up; nice strong legs that've always taken me where I want to go.

"What about practicing tonight?" I asked him. "You see your way clear to that? Or do you have plans?"

"I guess I can do that."

"I'll meet you at the studio tonight, ten o'clock, after I get off work." I gave him directions, and he had sense enough to go on his way then without a special look or smile.

Later I wondered what he'd been looking for in the Western Warehouse. I never did find out.

I spent that evening after work waiting for some message from Buck. He used to call Bill sometimes and ask him to take me word, and that old snake wasn't above adding his own twist: "Says he'll be home tomorrow but I never count my chickens before they hatch." But this time there was nothing. By midnight I'd have been glad to see even Bill's sorry face at the screen door.

Finally I got up and went down to the pay phones to call Fern. She's a night owl, I knew I wouldn't wake her. "Heard from Buck?" I asked, lining up quarters on the shelf.

"Not a word. I thought he'd call and cuss me out for turning Buddy in."

"You did the right thing. With that baby on the way, my boy has to grow up."

"Good luck!" I heard her inhaling. "What's on your mind, Mel?"

I ran my finger over the initials somebody had carved into the side of the phone. "I don't think Buck's coming home."

"What happened?"

"He wanted me to take Buddy and his girl in, make nice, start staying home, practice to be a grandma."

Fern didn't say anything. I knew she was sitting in the corner of her old purple couch, legs tucked up under her, cigarette hanging out of her mouth.

That voice started and I dropped three more quarters in.

"You still want him?" Fern asked.

That set me back on my heels. I thought of all the times Buck yelled at me, raised his fist—though he never had hit me and never would. He knew I wouldn't take that. Then I thought of his dead eyes when I told him about my dancing.

"I want him the way I want bread," I told her. "I don't even think about it. I guess we're broke to each other."

"So you going to quit dancing?"

"How do you know—"

"Buck said something last time he called. He doesn't like it, Mel. 'Course that foolishness in New York made it worse."

"Might as well ask me if I'm going to stop breathing."

And then we were both laughing, way in the middle of the night, Fern on her purple couch and me in the smelly, lighted-up phone booth, and I knew what I was telling her was the Gospel truth.

13

Rita's was packed next day with refugees from Indian Market, and by the time I got off, my feet were so swollen I thought I was never going to get them into the red boots. I begged two plastic bags from the kitchen, and they helped, though I knew I was going to have to take the bags off before I started dancing.

In the bathroom I put on more pancake, as much lipstick as my mouth could handle, and then the new red dress. All in all, I didn't look too bad.

Looks were the least of it, anyway.

Cutting through back streets, I got to the dance studio a little before ten. "I'm bringing in a live one," I told Monty; he was hunkered behind the desk, checking his messages. "You got space for us to practice?"

He looked at his schedule. Nobody can read it except Monty, though the instructors sometimes try. "We've got two lessons starting. There'll be room in the back." Then he looked at me. "Who is it, Mel?"

"Curiosity killed the cat," I told him, going to get the orange plastic cones they use to divide up the floor. They were stacked behind the rack of neon-colored dance dresses, and I thought, Some day I'll wear one of those.

Monty was into his next lesson, watching over his student's shoulder when Arthur came in the door. I was watching, too, from where I was sitting on the bench, and another of the instructors, Christopher, who was practicing turns, looked around, too, and so did Caroline, Two-Stepping a new client.

Arthur looked even taller than I'd remembered, and I felt that insane rush of pride, like I'd grown him myself—this total stranger.

I didn't waste much time on hellos. I planned to be as business-like as possible. "We'll start with the basic step," I told him, and I put him into position with a touch. I couldn't get over how comfortable it felt to lead him, big as he was, maybe because he didn't seem to know he was being led.

He had on black, polished boots, stovepipe jeans faded almost white, newer-looking denim shirt, but no bandana and no vest. It seemed like he knew where to draw the line.

I was instructing him in the traveling turn when Monty came over with his student on his arm—a roly-poly Hispanic woman I'd seen a couple of times. She had that dazed look, like she'd gone to heaven and was on the way back down.

Monty watched us closely. Then he took over and danced with Arthur, showing him the sweetheart position. Like all the instructors, Monty dances both the man's and the woman's part—I don't think it matters to him—but Arthur wasn't prepared for that, and he froze up.

Monty knew enough to turn him over to me. Then he whirled away with his day-dreaming student, looking around to see how I was going to undo the damage.

"It's a little early for the Sweetheart," I told Arthur. He was staring at me like a horse at a fire. "Let's go back to the basic step."

At first it was like shoving a refrigerator but after a while he loosened up.

"Monty's a good teacher," I told him, feeling my loyalty prick like a buried pin. "I'm just a beginner; he taught me everything I know."

"I don't want to dance with a man," Arthur told me. "I didn't come here for that."

I showed him the arm position for the traveling turn. "I'm sorry."

He tried to be gracious. "I guess he meant to help."

"That's it," I said, grateful. "You just hit the nail on the head. Monty doesn't know how to be uncomfortable on the dance floor, and he thinks it's that way for everybody."

I didn't tell him then—it was too soon—about the students I'd watched who were determined to misunderstand; three women and one man we didn't see at the studio anymore.

"From now on," I told Arthur, "I'll be your only instructor." I wondered how Monty was going to feel about that; probably all right, as long as there wasn't any money changing hands. "It'd be good if you'd sign up for a group lesson, though, dance with some other women for practice."

"I need to try the man's position, Mel," he said.

"For competing we'll have to do it that way," I said, changing the position of my arms. "This is going to work," I told him a minute later. He was responding to my back-leading like a kite lifting on a breeze.

Just don't call it following, I warned myself.

"Take each step like it's from your rib cage," I told him.

He tried it. It gave him a powerful long stride. Then I taught him about the target zone: where he should aim, stepping forward. Monty would never use a word like crotch, but that's what the target zone is, and it took Arthur a while to convince his right leg it ought to aim straight between mine.

Monty had decided it was time for music and he'd put on "One Part Be My Lover."

"Let's listen to the music, it's one of my favorite tunes," I said.

We were smoothing out our corners, learning how to turn them neatly.

"One part, go away," I sang.

I took a risk then and started teaching him the Rope Twist, which is definitely advanced. The Fiesta was less than two weeks off, and I wanted him to be ready with at least a few fancy steps.

"You're doing real good," I told him at the end of an hour. "Thank you for being willing to do this. I think you'll be ready in two weeks, at least if you can see your way to meeting me here every couple of days."

"I'll make the time," he told me.

"Hey, that's great." He sounded grim, and I wanted to keep it light. "I've got to get along home now, but why don't you stay and watch the next class, pick up some pointers?"

"You want me to?"

Only a big man can say that.

"Yes, I do. You'll learn something."

He sat down on the bench, meek as a lamb.

Monty ran over to meet me at the door. "You signed up for Albuquerque?"

"Signed up and paid, too. Amounted to two weeks of tip money, just like that."

"You going to take him?"

"That's my plan."

"You know they won't let you lead."

I sighed. "You going to tell on me?"

"I won't need to. The judges will notice, first thing."

"Women back-lead all the time and get away with it."

He'd told me that, himself.

109

"Just don't dress him up in a three-tier skirt," he said, and I thought, Monty doesn't like this, and for reasons that don't have anything to do with who's leading. But he was smiling.

"Maybe I don't want to win any prizes, Monty. Maybe I just want to dance, once in my life, the way that suits me," I said.

It was only partly a lie. I did want to win prizes, some day, lots of them, but the leading was more important now.

Monty followed me out into the parking lot. "It won't work, Mel. Think about it."

"I will," I said, going off to my car under an evening sky darkening toward a storm, big clouds piling up over the Sangres.

Goddamnit, I thought, what's Monty going to do to stop me? Step out there on the floor at Albuquerque and grab me? Holler through a bull horn, "This woman is trying to lead"? What can the judges do except ignore me?

I looked back. The studio was a lighted fish tank, bright-colored couples floating in the florescence. Arthur was still sitting on the bench—I could see his broad back—elbows on his knees, like a high school jock lost in an English class.

I went on home, my feet like two raw hamburgers inside those plastic bags I'd forgotten in the excitement to take off.

As soon as I drove in, I saw Buck's pickup in its usual spot.

His suitcase wasn't out where he always put it, on the kitchen table. Leaving, when he does it out in the open, is always a big deal, and when he does it on the sly, deep at night, it's a big deal, too; where he puts the suitcase marks the difference.

Instead, there was a bunch of snapshots spread out around the salt and pepper, and Buck was coming out of our bedroom with another bunch in his hands.

"Where've you been?" I asked. He didn't answer me.

"Look here," he said instead, like I'd been gone about a minute.

I looked. The snapshots were old faded color, taken by somebody with no talent. There were groups, backs of heads, some child's birthday party, the candle flames looking like smears, and a woman on a porch swing with a child snuggled in under her arm.

"Why are you showing me these now?" I asked.

"It's time," Buck said. "Past time, probably."

"For what?"

"For you to see these. I got to thinking, driving around. I know your past, at least part of it, the part that's Buddy. It's time for you to know mine."

"What opened you up?"

"That baby coming. I started remembering."

I studied the snapshot. "Who's that?"

"Hilda. Denver, sometime in the early seventies. I rented a two-up-two-down with a shingle roof. Working for the Model Cities Program, building houses for a bunch of down-and-outs."

"Who's the child?"

"Sammy," he said. "My son," he added heavily. "You said you wanted to know."

"I can't remember saying that. But you're right, I've wanted to know for years."

"You never asked."

"Maybe I was scared to find out," I said, and then I took the snapshot and studied it. Nice face, Hilda; new perm, wearing what we used to call a housedress, with little checks. The boy looked like the apple of her eye, the way she was smiling down at him. "You never divorced her, did you?" I'd known that for a long time.

"How'd you know that?"

"Your secrets. The things you try to hide. After a while, they stick out like barbed wire."

"I was married to her more than twenty years ago."

"They had divorces, the way I hear it, back then."

He shrugged, looking away, his face creased. "I couldn't do it, Mel. We had too much past between us."

"What happened to Sammy?"

"I don't know. She didn't want me to see him. I lost touch."

"He looks about four, here. So you never saw him after you lit out."

"Hilda wanted money. I didn't have any after I quit—"

"Quit, or was fired?"

"I was drinking. It was nip and tuck for a while there, after I left Denver."

"Didn't you write her?"

"I didn't want her to know where to find me."

"So, all these years, no birthday card, no nothing."

"Don't rub it in, Mel. The way I saw it, I had no choice. After they sacked me—"

"What'd you do?"

"Had words with one of the foremen."

"So it goes." I started leafing through the collection of snap-shots: Hilda, younger and fresher-looking in a candy-striped play suit on a beach somewhere. Looking sleepy in a housecoat with a lump of new baby in her arms. Leaning over to light the candles on the cake, or worn out, standing next to a Christmas tree with too much on it. A homemaker, it looked like, a woman who probably said her prayers on her knees by the bed at night, then got in to do whatever her husband wanted. "I don't know why you left," I said. "These look like the whole nine yards."

Buck was standing behind me. He put his hand on my shoulder. "I was a kid, I didn't understand. I thought I loved her."

"How do you know you didn't?" I still halfway believed the trap-pings meant something. I mean, somebody had to finance the tree and the birthday cake and the gingham housedress; somebody had to put his shoulder to the wheel, to keep the whole thing going.

He gathered up the pictures. "Because as soon as she started asking for things, I wanted out. Wanted it bad.

"Love. All that. I was giving it to her, I thought, but not with words or show. She wanted words and show. After a while she wouldn't take anything else."

"You miss the boy?" I asked.

"I don't know him, how can I miss him? He was always her lap baby, anyway." He looked at me, measuring. "Sometimes I do feel like I miss something I've never even had."

"You going to look for them?"

He shook his head slowly. "Too late, Mel. I don't want to mess up their lives. I expect Hilda's been remarried for years. And if that's so, Sammy's been raised by another man, maybe believes he's his dad."

"How come you never told me, all this time?"

"You had Buddy," he said. "I thought for a while there I'd have Buddy, too. When it didn't work out, I just didn't see the point of dragging all this in. There wasn't a thing you could have done."

I said, "I'll go down to El Paso with you if you can wait a couple of days."

"I'll call them and see."

That was the quickest, if not the easiest, agreement we'd ever reached.

"I can't go right off," I said. I had some dancing to do before I went to deal with what everybody else would call my Real Life: my son, his girlfriend, their baby, my ex-lover, his wife—all that.

But Buck was already on the phone to El Paso, and he must have got Paul's answering machine (I hardly believed the man I'd known in the 60s even had an answering machine) because he was leaving the kind of message people only leave on machines, crisp and sure: "We'll be down this weekend."

Eat my cake and have it too, I thought, that's what I want, like always. And for once, the little voice that usually warns me, "You can't do that, not and get away with it," choked off after a mutter. Maybe my luck was changing.

I went into our bedroom to take off my dance clothes, and Buck followed. He watched me like he'd never seen me undress before, and I knew he was going to say something about my new red boots.

He picked one up and studied it. "Pretty."

"They're required, for Albuquerque."

"When's that?"

"Less than two weeks. I'll be gone most of that weekend. My first competition," I told him, swelling a little. "Monty says I'm ready." I didn't tell him I'd finally found a willing partner.

He set the boot down. "I believe I could see my way to driving you down there."

"You won't be able to dance, and I don't see you sitting around hour after hour, watching."

He ran his hands down his thighs like he was wiping something off. "I thought maybe you'd like me to go."

"Next time," I said. "The first time I may be too nervous. You could throw me off my stride." I zipped my jeans and went to see if there was there anything to eat.

Buck was right behind me.

I studied the inside of the refrigerator. It was bare except for two withered apples and three cans of beer.

"I'm trying to say I'm sorry," he told me, touching my shoulder.

"For what?"

"Leaving."

"I never have tried to tie you down."

He looked at me. It was true and not true, both.

"How about we order in pizza? I know it's late, but I'm starved."

He didn't say anything, and I finally turned around and looked at him. Right off, I caught his shame the way I'd catch a cold, sitting next to somebody who's sneezing. "Oh God," I said. "Not this. I don't need this." I closed the refrigerator door and leaned back against it.

"You're always pushing me, Mel," he said. "Taking that petition around—"

"Fat lot of good that did—"

"—embarrassing me with Bill and the neighbors. Acting like a stone when Buddy came, hardly even looking at his girl—"

"How do I know she's not just another piece of trash?"

"—letting me sneak off whenever I get the urge—"

"So that's my fault, too? A man who's going to cat is going to cat."

"Mel," he said, gripping my shoulders, "don't you know all you'd ever have to do is ask me to stay?"

"What is this?" I shrugged, trying to get his hands off, but they stayed tight as crab claws on my shoulders. "I'm the one who decides what you do?"

"You never let on you cared. A man needs to know that."

I laughed. More a bark than a laugh. "I'm here, aren't I? It's been more than ten years—"

"I know there're others, Mel," he said.

"Others?"

"Men."

I sat down like a sack at the dinette table. "I just wish there was."

Buck was standing over me. "Tell me the truth. I'm not going to hit you."

"I think I found me a dance partner, one that'll let me lead." I threw it out like bait for a bear.

"So that's it," he said. "I always knew it was."

"Was what?"

"Your dancing. Putting in all that time, spending all that money. It looks like to me there must be cheaper ways to find a fuck."

"The way you do, in bars?" I stood up when I said it. We were at a draw. In the old movies, this is the time the hands start reaching for the holsters.

"I just do what I have to do," Buck said. I could see sweat starting to bead on his forehead. "Considering."

"Considering what? I never turn you down, in bed."

"No, you just don't care what I do. The last time I got back from a little road trip, you never even asked me where I'd been."

"I'm tired of asking, Buck. I already know the answer."

"Which is?"

"Nowhere. Nothing."

He turned away, shaking his head.

"How about we order pizza?" I asked again. "I'm still starving."

Which is how we ended the day—sitting at the dinette table with a big wheel of pepperoni and extra cheese between us.

Not peace, maybe, but the quiet of the draw.

~ 14 ~

The girl's father, Bridget's father, this rich man Mr. Spencer McCain from the Delta, had charm down to a science. I blushed more that weekend in El Paso than I have since I turned thirteen.

Forget I'd gone to El Paso with some notion of having it out with Bridget's parents: this baby on the way, and what were they prepared to do about it? Forget we'd driven most of the way without saying a word, Buck mad as hell over the nights I'd spent out practicing with Arthur, no excuses or explanations given or asked for. Forget the way our life, Buck's and mine, was stuck like a big lump of unchewed bread in my throat.

I say forget because I did forget, soon as I saw that big brick house on the ridge over El Paso. Buck said one word, "Money," but money didn't tell the whole story: what had happened to Paul in the thirty years since I left him hanging onto the edge of a bar in Taos?

His house looked like it'd been put down on the ridge yesterday, trees, driveway, old-time lamp posts—all bought at the same time and assembled. There wasn't a brown leaf or a dried-up bloom in the big flower bed.

The grass in that big yard must have used half the water in the county to keep that shade of green, and there was an urn—I swear it—on the porch, full of ivy and pink geraniums.

"Did somebody see all this in their mind before it happened?" I asked, and before Buck could answer, I said, "I know anyhow it wasn't Paul."

"Somebody sure signed a lot of checks," Buck said.

"Where'd her money come from—this wife of Paul's?"

He shrugged.

"Used to be he carried everything he owned in a duffel bag," I said. "Whiskers down to his collarbone, hair down to his shoulder blades. Now an urn full of ivy and geraniums."

I parked the pickup next to one of those new-bought trees. Buck got out of his side and came around to open my door. "Give them a chance, Mel," he said.

"They already have every chance they could hope for," I said, hopping down.

Neither of us had dressed up, and as soon as we stepped on that brick porch, I was glad we hadn't. My jeans and denim shirt were clean but not pressed—who has time or taste for ironing?—and Buck looked like he might have slept one night in what he had on.

Buck punched the bell set deep as a navel in the wood beside the door.

There was a commotion inside like a herd of wolves let loose.

I said, "Sounds like they have an army of guard dogs on duty." Then I turned around and looked down at the big ugly city, a mass of buildings and throughways sprawled across the valley under a fog of sunburned exhaust and factory fumes.

Then the door opened and the army bounded out. Buck and I stood our ground while those dogs leaped and snarled. Meantime a skinny old man was shouting commands that didn't mean a thing to that herd. All he needed, really, was a stick.

Finally he got his hand on the ringleader's collar and dragged him growling into the hall, and the rest of them followed. While he was kicking the stragglers through the door, I looked at the side of his face and saw it was Paul.

Spindle-shanked, humped shoulders, loose pants falling down below his belly, looking like a man who'd spent his working life behind a desk and now was put out to pasture.

"What happened?" I wanted to ask this man I'd lived with for two years and borne a son to, but Buck got in my way, sticking out his hand.

Paul turned around. His skin was yellow and his teeth were, too, when he smiled, shaking my husband's hand.

"He used to look so god-forsaken young," I said, still surprised.

He looked at me, finally. I waited for the double-take: thirty years, after all. "Melanie?"

"I guess I finally look grown-up enough for my whole name."

He studied me till I wanted to put my hands over my face.

"How many years is it?" Buck asked.

Paul didn't know and I had to figure to come up with a number. "Somewhere between twenty-seven and twenty-eight. Buddy was two when I . . ." It failed me, to finish that sentence.

"Lit out," Paul said, and grinned me a sideways grin that proved he was still there, somewhere.

"Best thing I ever did for you," I told him, and then all three of us found our way to a laugh. "Look how your luck has changed." But underneath I was thinking, The whole center of life, used up and gone.

"You're looking well," Paul said, measuring his words.

"If you said I was looking good, I'd know you were lying."

He smiled. "Come on in and have a drink."

We went into a big room crowded with brand-new furniture.

"You expecting a convention?" I asked. There was a bunch of arranged flowers on every table and a platform, lighted up, at the end.

"Emily had her group here yesterday," Paul explained, like everybody we knew had groups and a place to entertain them. Before I could ask what group, Emily herself came in the door behind us.

I knew she was there before I turned around because of her perfume, one of those lemony scents that comes in a plain bottle and costs an arm and a leg.

She was not a young woman.

I'll give you that, Paul, I thought. You didn't go for a young chick to warm your bones.

Paul's wife held out her hand. When I took it, I felt lines and ridges. "You do your own digging?" I asked, thinking about that perfect garden.

"The only reason to have garden." She didn't smile; she was looking at me straight.

"I want her to hire somebody," Paul said. "Mexican gardeners are a dime a dozen around here. She's going to get a stroke, working out there all day in the sun." He said this to Buck, like they—men, husbands—must share a view.

"Only good reason," Emily said, like this was something I was sure to understand: bone-breaking labor, done for the love of sweat.

"I'm a waitress," I told her. "When I get back from work, I sit down in front of the TV—" which wasn't always true, but I wanted her to get a taste of my life, right off.

"Paul told me. You pay your own bills, make your own way."

Buck laughed softly. I knew he was thinking about my dancing lessons, my red boots.

Emily wiped her hands on her thighs, and I caught sight of a sizable diamond on that hand. I knew there was more to her story than a love of stoop labor.

Paul went to one of those trays on legs and started pouring drinks. I remembered he had a habit of not asking what anybody wanted. He brought me a glass of whiskey, warm: two good inches, and it was three o'clock in the afternoon.

"You moved on from beer," I said.

"Mississippi people like their sour mash," somebody said behind me, and I looked around and saw the man who turned out to be Bridget's father.

He walked over at a stroll, like he was taking the measure, by foot, of a good rug.

"You're Mel," he said, opening a pair of eyes wide as pansies.

"Who told you to call me by my short name?" I asked while he massaged my hand.

"I don't rightly remember," he said.

"That's Spencer," Paul said, bringing his drink. "Bridget's pa."

Emily was over by one of the tables, adjusting a bloom, and I guessed she'd already gotten a snootful of the man from Mississippi.

Buck said, "I've been looking forward to meeting you." and they shook.

"My bride'll be down directly—" aiming his drawl at me.

"You just get married?" I asked.

"Thirty-five years come June first, and I wish it'd been twice as long." He wasn't ruffled, maybe couldn't be—the kind of man who turns every remark into a compliment.

"Where are the young people?" he asked Paul, who was already drifting over to the tray for a refill. "They're the cause of this get-together." He winked and flashed at me.

"The five of us certainly wouldn't be in the same room otherwise," I said.

Paul had his back to us, fiddling with bottles. Emily was still busy with her flowers. Buck was behind me—I could feel him a few inches from my spine.

"I believe they're in the kitchen, eating breakfast," Emily said.

The rest of us started toward a swinging door; Paul led the way, and Buck held the door.

We passed through a long room crowded with glass-fronted cabinets. At the end, a big kitchen opened out. And there they were, our two, soon to be our three, sitting at the table.

I saw the back of my boy's head, and my throat seized up. I wanted to lay my hand on his light-colored hair I hadn't touched in so long.

The girl, Bridget, set down her cup and looked at me. Then her eyes slid off to Paul. He was the newest ingredient in her concoction, the one with the oddest flavor.

"Here we are," Paul said, like maybe we needed name tags. "Here we all are."

"Not quite all," Emily said behind him, and then she called out a few words in Spanish, and a woman in a white uniform with a baby in her arms came.

Emily held out her arms and the nurse put the baby in them. The baby was staring at the rest of us. He had one of those electric light bulb faces, long and rounded and full of white light.

Paul went to the counter and started to pour coffee into rose-colored cups, and the nurse passed them around, asking us whether we wanted sugar and cream. It was real cream, thick enough to need spooning out of the little silver pitcher.

We all started talking at once, then all stopped and laughed, except for Buddy. He was concentrating on chewing his toast.

Then Bridget stood up and gave me a dry little kiss. She smelled like a good clean child—soap, talcum powder, shampoo. "I'm glad you came," she said, her big firm belly pressing into me.

"That baby must be about ready to pop," I said.

The other baby was looking at me. He had a big thatch of dark hair and two eyes round and brown as shoe buttons. I wondered where he'd come from; he didn't look like anything I'd seen in that house.

"We adopted him in Guatemala," Emily explained. "Let's take our coffee to the living room." The nurse took the baby away.

There in the long room with its tables and flowers, another middle-aged woman was waiting for us, arms akimbo, wearing purple pants and a top to match, with fringe around the bottom.

Spencer went right to her and put his arm around her waist. "This is Daisy," he said, and I knew already that had to be his wife's name.

She went around the circle, shaking hands. When she got to Bridget, she smiled, and I dropped my arm. She was claiming this girl, by blood right if nothing else. "How are you?" she asked like she hadn't seen her daughter in a few years.

"All right, Mama." Bridget sounded polite, obliged.

"Good. You've gained a lot of weight," Daisy said, and all of a sudden Buddy was there, putting himself between Daisy and Bridget.

"Her doctor told her to gain," he said.

We settled like a flock of birds on Emily's stiff chairs. There wasn't a soft spot, a broken-down couch or swayback armchair in the entire room.

The silence was hard on us, so I turned to Emily, perched next to me, and asked about her baby.

She fielded my question like she heard it at least once every day. "I was past menopause when I met Paul, so we decided to adopt. There's a terrible situation in Guatemala, pregnant girls having their babies in ditches, practically."

Buddy said, "Markie's young enough to play with ours, later on." He didn't exactly say it to me, but he didn't leave me out, either. It was the first time I'd heard him mention his baby, like it existed for him, already, and that was the exact moment it began to exist for me—not a problem, not something to be fixed or solved, but a little soul already among us.

Then Daisy asked him, "What are your plans, exactly?" She was still hugging her arms like she was freezing to death.

"They're staying here till after the baby comes," Emily said, before Buddy had to answer.

"And after that?" Daisy asked, still arrowing in on Buddy.

"They're welcome to come up to Santa Fe," Buck said, just as Buddy was opening his mouth.

Daisy didn't seem to hear. She was looking at Buddy like he'd failed her one and only test.

"We've found a place for them," Buck went on, and he reached across the space between our chairs and took my hand. "Me and Granny here are kind of looking forward to some baby-sitting."

"Speak for yourself, John," I said, and the rest of them laughed.

"Where's this place you've found?" Buddy asked, and this time he looked straight at Buck for the first time since we came.

"The people next door to us moved out," Buck told him.

"Not yet they haven't," I said.

"Not the trailer park." Daisy's voice was broom straw dry.

"They couldn't afford an apartment, the way rents are in Santa Fe," Buck said.

"What we're going to need is help with the baby," Buddy explained, and this time he looked at me. "Somebody to give bottles, and things."

"We can manage that," Buck said.

"I thought you didn't want us anywhere near you." Buddy was looking at me.

Buck squeezed my hand. "Your mom here talks a tough game, but when it gets right down to it, she has a heart the size of—"

"I don't want to offer more than I can give," I told my son.

Spencer started saying I'd feel entirely different as soon as I saw the baby, or held her, anyway.

Maybe I won't, I thought. Maybe I won't see her, or hold her, if they decide to stay here.

Daisy said, "You see what you're taking on. Two young people, too very young people, with no way to support themselves—"

"Daisy," Spencer said, almost gruff.

She flared out at him then. "We're not going to give them money. It's totally irresponsible."

Buck squeezed my hand. "We'll help them," he said. "We don't have much but what we do have—"

"No!" Daisy's voice cut through his. "I won't allow it—keeping them babies forever."

Buddy said, "We don't want money. What we want is grandparents."

"You'll have them, in Santa Fe," Buck promised him.

"New Orleans, too," Spencer said, fast.

This time, Daisy didn't even need to look at him. We all knew New Orleans meant her house, and she made the rules there.

"You can tell that Monsignor of yours to perform a baptism," Spencer told her. "Get something back for all that money."

"The Church doesn't baptize bastards," Daisy said. Bridget made a sound like she'd been hit across the chest, a fast let-out of air.

Emily said, "We'd offer, if it wasn't for Markie. We've got our hands full."

Paul stood up, then. I recognized his look: something was fomenting inside him. I remembered one night long ago when he'd thrown a boot at Buddy's crib because he wouldn't stop crying.

He stalked over to the window. Outside, the nurse was pushing baby Markie in a carriage as big as a small car.

"Well," Spencer said, and he leaned over and gave Daisy a peck, "it looks like we've got us a plan, here."

"What is it?" Bridget asked.. "What are we going to do?"

Buddy stared at her. Their future was floating in the air above their heads, and Spencer was about to grab it down.

"You're coming back to Santa Fe with us," Buck said, fast, and I loved and hated him for that, about equally.

"Maybe that is the best plan," Spencer said, like he was just now making up his mind. "Everybody else is so damn busy." I knew he'd understood his wife didn't want them.

"But my granddaughter can't grow up in a trailer park," Daisy said.

"It matters?" I asked. "You just called her a bastard."

"Your son needs to marry my daughter," Daisy told me. The words tasted bad but she had to say them. "It's the least he can do."

"So she'll have a name," Emily said.

Buddy said, low, "I guess that's none of your business," and Bridget let out something that sounded like a mew.

Then Paul started. He was standing behind me, and when I heard that tone, I knew he was Paul, still, the frail boy with the angel face and the cracking snake-whip temper. "Mel's not taking this baby! She's taken one baby already. Enough is enough!"

I turned around. "I guess you mean I took Buddy," I said.

"Stole him in the middle of the night. Never even left me a note, phone number—nothing!"

"I didn't want you coming after us."

"I didn't know where my son was till he was eighteen years old."

"I don't see what all that has to do with the problem we're facing now," Daisy said.

"She's not taking my grandchild, too," Paul said. "She's not robbing me a second time."

"I took Buddy away because I thought you were going to hurt him," I said.

He settled down, then. I'd played my top card.

"I was just trying to survive," I told the rest of them, knowing that word was packed full of meanings. "Trying to keep me and my baby safe. Paul was drinking hard, and he had a devil of a temper."

Paul crumpled. Fuming, muttering, he stumbled over to the bar tray for a refill.

"Now it's settled," Spencer said, "I believe I'll go up and take my nap."

Everybody started to file out of the room. I went along, too. I wanted what I knew I'd find at the top of the stairs: a big spare room, shades drawn, air-conditioner humming. I wanted to take off my jeans and lie down, pretend, even, that everything was settled to my satisfaction.

Buck wouldn't let it go at that. "This is going to change everything," he said, heaving himself onto the bed beside me.

"Take off your shoes. This is a satin bedspread."

He did.

"Money always changes everything," he said.

I turned on my side away from him and closed my eyes. I didn't want to hear.

15

Next day, at the top of La Bajada Hill, with Santa Fe spread out in the valley below us, Buck told me again he was sorry.

I said, "You're setting some kind of a record."

"I know this has messed up your plans."

"This?"

"Them coming," he said, ducking his head. There'd been a long phone call, plans had been made without consulting me.

"I'm still going to Albuquerque next Friday for Fiesta," I said.

He looked at me. "That's the day they'll be getting here, Mel."

"You fixed that with them. I didn't have a thing to do with it. Was in the bathroom at the time, if I remember correctly."

He shook his head. "It'll take us about a week to

get ready for them, rent the space from Bill, find them a—"

"Which makes it next Friday. And next Friday is Albuquerque. You knew that, Buck." I was gripping the steering wheel tight but it was sliding through my sweaty hands. I pulled out to pass an eighteen-wheeler and accelerated down the long hill into town. The pickup started bucking the way it does going over eighty.

"Slow down, Mel." He hated to be the one to say it. "The cops are always out on this stretch."

"Speed limit's seventy-five." I was going ninety. "Besides, they're all your buddies, they aren't going to write us any tickets." I pressed the accelerator to the floor and Buck started putting on the brakes on his side.

"For God's sake, Mel."

"Least I can do, the way you've tried to take my life out of my hands." But I slowed down. Our exit was coming up.

He sat quiet then, staring at the car dealerships on Cerrillos, colored flags flying.

"You're not going to hang around to change that baby's diapers," I told him. "Just about the time I get home from work, you'll be ready to light out. Sure, you'll slap a twenty on the table, on your way." I braked to make the turn into our park. Bill was standing by the mailboxes like he was watching for us. I didn't even wave.

"I'm sorry, Mel," Buck said again. "It just seemed like the right thing to do. Still does."

I tore up the gravel to the Wilderness. The lot next door was empty, the hook-ups hanging forlorn.

Bill walked over and rapped on the window. Buck rolled it down.

"Glad to see you're back," Bill said.

Buck muttered something.

"Marty and Jean hauled out of here sometime this afternoon,"

Bill told us. "They're going down to her folks in Truth or Consequences, park that thing in the back yard." He leaned around Buck to look at me. "I don't want no trouble."

"Her son's coming next Friday, with his girlfriend," Buck said. "They're expecting a baby in a couple of months."

"You going to wedge them in your place?"

"Well, I thought maybe you and I could talk."

I jumped out my side of the pickup and left them there. "Just don't let him hike up the rent for that space," I called back to Buck. "I know what Marty and Jean paid."

Then I unlocked the door to the Wilderness. I'd forgotten the way we'd left it, dirty clothes heaped on the dinette table, waiting to go to the Laundromat, dishes piled in the sink. The faucet was dripping and the whole place smelled ripe from garbage left to ferment in the pail under the sink. I sniffed, remembering Emily's big white kitchen and, further back, my mother's house in the Purchase with her row of polished copper pots and her curtains printed with geraniums.

My roots are starting to catch up with me, I thought, and I saw roots running their feet off across the desert. I'd better be careful. It's down-payment time, and I want to be sure I go on putting my money on my own life.

Mrs. Lopez had given me two days off to go to El Paso for a "family emergency" on condition I give her two extra evenings when we got back, so as soon as I was inside the Wilderness, I started pulling off my jeans. I had a dance lesson with Monty at ten PM, so I put on my leotard and my practice skirt, figuring I'd change to my waitress get-up at work.

Bill was walking away and Buck was coming toward the Wilderness when I stepped out the door. He took one look at me and said, "You're not going to work like that."

"I'll change into my uniform when I get there. This is for dance class, later."

I went to pass him and he grabbed my elbow. "Not with your legs showing all the way up to your crotch."

"My waitress get-up is just as short," I said.

He didn't let go of my elbow. "I've just about had it with all this, Mel."

"Go ahead and have it, then." I didn't care what I said. I didn't even care what he did. It was all one to me now.

He dropped his hand. I flew like something let go.

"You don't care," he said from some empty place deep in his chest. "I don't believe you ever did care."

My right hand was on the pickup door. I spoke into my reflection in the shut window and I couldn't help noticing I was looking pretty good. "You're wrong there, Buck. I used to care a lot."

"What happened?"

"I guess I finally found out what matters to me."

"And that's not me, it looks like."

I got in the pickup and rolled down my window. It wasn't like Buck to make himself pitiful. "I'm not going to honor that," I said. "You know the way I've always felt about you."

Buck didn't move. "It was just one boy," he said. "I want you to know that, now."

"One boy what?"

"One son I lost. It was just Sammy."

I sighed so deep it heaved my belly. "Tell me later, Buck. You waited ten years, you can wait a few more hours."

He held up his hand, then let it fall. I never had known Buck to act that way. He stepped back toward the Wilderness like I might mash him on the way out.

Grandpa, I thought, maybe that's it—feeling old in his own way, all his muscles loosening. But I guessed it wasn't just that. Something had touched him, opened him up.

Work was slow, Indian Market over and the summer beginning

finally to wind down. We still had the burning of Zozobra to look forward to, but that's mostly for locals, and Rita's depends on tourists.

Mrs. Lopez was in a foul mood. She snapped at me about quitting fifteen minutes early, which I had to do to get to the studio on time. I didn't care. She was short on wait staff, and I was good. She wasn't going to fire me, not yet, anyway.

Our new bartender, Franny, watched me putting on my practice skirt; she was taking her break, smoking a cigarette. in the locker room. She's so quick at getting the drink orders right and remembering people's names even Mrs. Lopez has to cut her some slack.

"I used to dance, before I got married," she told me.

"Marriage'll do it, every time," I said.

"You're married," she said.

"Yeah, but he hasn't yanked the leash yet," I told her. "He's fixing to any day now."

"What're you going to do?"

"One thing I'm not going to do is quit dancing."

She watched me going out like she thought I had the world on a string. Of course I wasn't as sure as I sounded. Whoever is?

Monty was in a bad mood, and I remembered reading in the paper there was an eclipse of the moon that night. Maybe that was why all the chickens had their tail feathers ruffled. I don't believe in that kind of thing more than half, but sometimes half is enough.

He told me he'd been teaching thirteen hours straight and his back was killing him. He was leaning against the wall when I came in, shoveling down a bag of chips, those blond dreadlocks hanging down around his face like seaweed.

"That your supper?" I asked.

He nodded. Monty doesn't care what he eats; he has every woman in the studio worrying about his diet. They bring him fresh fruit, or little homemade casseroles.

We started out with the Two-Step. That dance looks simple,

but it's not, particularly when you add all the gewgaws you need for competition.

I was having trouble with my timing; my slow steps were too quick, and my quick steps were too slow.

Monty started sorting me out, counting the beats. I was working hard when I caught sight of myself in the long mirror. My practice skirt was flaring out, and my red boots were flashing. God, I looked good.

"Better," Monty said—his highest praise. He hooked my hand over his arm, going to the glory hole to change the CD. "You practicing with Arthur?"

He looked at me. Monty usually keeps his eyes to himself, or concentrates on some distant spot.

"What?" I asked. My heart was sinking, fast.

"You can't lead at Fiesta."

"The way I do it, nobody's going to know. I take the woman's position. Just a little light pressure—"

"The judges'll know. They'll disqualify you."

"For leading? There's a rule?"

He snapped a CD into place. "You can't do it, Mel."

"I'll take the risk."

"You're there to represent the studio."

"My God, Monty, listen—"

"I've listened enough. It's okay here, nobody cares. But at Fiesta, my reputation's on the line. The judges see you leading, they'll think I never taught you the difference."

"So I'll wear a sign saying you taught me the right way only I'm insisting on doing it wrong."

"Not funny, Mel." The music started—Bonnie's "Nick of Time"—and he led me out on the floor.

We flew around the room, practicing turns, and I started to remember: "My parents used to turn back the rug when there was a Big Band show on the radio and dance, for hours, it seemed like. Broadcast live from the beautiful Roof Garden of the Chicago Hotel."

Monty was working on my arms, turning my hands in, then out, so he could catch my wrist and twirl me. Then he showed me a lowering step, right foot back, with an extended arm—"Like you're picking an apple," he explained.

I said, "You know something, Monty? I want to make you proud. I want to see that written in those red bead lights."

"You're dancing better," Monty said. It was high praise.

"One thing," he said when we were drinking water out of little paper cups at the cooler, "you're never going to lead me."

"I wouldn't even try," I said, glad he'd forgotten.

"I guess Arthur doesn't know enough to ask questions."

"He's just a beginner, but he's coming along fast."

"So I noticed." He led me out on the floor again and started me on the Cha-Cha, probably my least favorite. When Monty's leading me through it, though, I don't much care what dance I do.

What is it about a good lead?

I've asked some of the other women at the studio: Lolly, who's about my age, a retired schoolteacher finally free to kick up her heels, and Emma, a technician at the hospital who used to seem scared, and Joy, who makes silver buckles to sell at the Flea. They all just smile and shake their heads, like I'd ask them why they wear perfume or chose ruby-red nail polish.

A good lead is like that—something we all love and don't want to talk about. I might as well have asked those women about sex, straight out. Well, there it is: magic. I hate to say it, I don't believe in that kind of thing, anymore than I believe in the effects of an eclipse of the moon, but seeing it is something else. Feeling it, too.

And then, a good lead's so rare.

With most men, all you get is their good intentions. They don't do anything to you or for you, except hold you in a limp kind of way. They don't want to get close, for one thing. Maybe that's left over from when they were boys and used to get hard-ons, dancing, and embarrass themselves.

Some few put too much into it; they pull you around, almost ask you to fight back. The worst of them count the beats when you don't need them to and tell you what foot to start on, when all women know it's always the right. They don't lead with their bodies: God forbid! Don't seem to know they have bodies. I wonder if it's the fault of their mothers, slapping their hands, training them not to touch.

I've heard Monty call what he does "leading from the core." He doesn't depend much on words, but when he's driven to it, he'll say that. Trouble is, a man has to have a core to lead from, and be willing to use it.

Have we taken that away from them, we new-fangled women? Taken their lead away? (And here I was, ready to do it for real.) Somehow that sounds like an excuse, to me. You can't take something away a man doesn't know he has.

No—we're trying to fill the gap, or at least, I was.

But I did remember—I told Monty this—watching my father waltz my mother around the living room, the radio blaring, the little house and the little town it sat in sinking below the horizon. It seemed to me he could lead.

Monty didn't say anything to that. He was through with me—my hour was over—and looking at Lolly, his next student, sitting on the bench pulling on her black dancing boots. Monty switches his attention fast, it's like a searchlight swiveling.

The Wilderness was pitch dark when I got back, all the lights off, and I was glad. The last thing I wanted was more words with Buck.

I dove into the bed with every stitch on, too tired even to use the bathroom. Buck was sleeping like a stone.

Toward dawn, he threw his arm over me, and I woke up. Outside our little window, the full moon looked milky with a black shadow creeping over it. I stayed awake 'til the shadow passed and the moon shone out again.

And I knew my time was coming. Coming fast.

Next evening after work I went straight to the studio to practice with Arthur. He was catching on, maybe too fast—one of those rare men who seems to have dancing in his blood. I didn't want him going too fast; that's when the questions start.

Monty was watching us from over by the desk, talking on the telephone and giving orders to Sylvia, who deals with the business side.

I led Arthur through the first part of the Two-Step, my arms in the woman's position, leading him with gentle pressure the way I'd seen Caroline doing when she was teaching her men students. "So tell me a little about yourself," I said when we were underway, to distract him from counting the beat. "How come you want to learn to dance?"

He was concentrating too hard, but he loosened up then. "My older sister's a professional dancer, back East. I always wanted to learn."

"She teach you?"

"No. I didn't know any boys who danced, back then, didn't want to seem like a freak. Now, I don't care."

I remembered Monty telling me he rode his bike ten miles every afternoon after school, to take his lesson, how he wheedled his way into the girls' ballet class, even though the kids made fun of him. I wondered if maybe Arthur had that kind of drive. You don't find it too often.

"How come you don't care now?" I asked him.

"I guess I grew up finally and thought, To hell with it, I want to learn to dance and I'm going to."

He was ready to go on with more of his life story, but I didn't need it. "Let's talk about what we're going to wear," I said, maneuvering him into a turn. "You got a hat, and boots?"

He smiled. We were in Sweetheart, pacing along together like old-time lovers. "First things I bought when I got here from Detroit a year ago was a hat and boots. Felt like a fool when I wore them, threw them in the back of the closet."

He sounded like Buck, except Buck would have known better

than to spend all that money. "Well, you need to get them out now," I told him. "Boots and a hat are required. Black?"

"Sure."

"I'm going to wear black, too."

It took a little while for that to sink in. "We're going to match?"

"Yes, Arthur, we're going to match," I said. "And you and I are the only ones who're going to know which is which."

He thought that was a joke.

Later, driving home, I beat my hands on the steering wheel and shouted out loud for pure joy. Things were starting to go my way. I wasn't used to that, but I was prepared to make the adjustment.

I ducked my head to the big white moon, hanging up above the Sangres like a visible blessing; there's something, I thought, to paying your dues. A day dawns when everything's paid off and you're free to step out.

A lot of life had gone by first.

Buck was waiting for me in the dinette, sitting at the table. He didn't have the newspaper, or a beer. He was just sitting.

"Something's happened, Mel," he said as soon as I walked in the door.

I dropped my purse on the table. "Tell me quick."

"Buddy got picked up, on the way here from El Paso. Driving too fast. They checked with the computer, found out he's breaking probation in Texas. They took him down to detention."

A minute ago I'd thought I was free.

"What do we do now?"

"Nothing," Buck said. "There's nothing we can do. Judge already decided no bail. They'll send him back to Texas to stand trial on some old drug charges, soon as the paperwork's done."

"Bridget?"

"She turned right around and drove back to El Paso. Called me from there."

"Went to Paul."

"Looks like it. Spencer and Daisy are back in Mississippi."

"Can I see Buddy?"

"Don't know. Not tonight, anyway. You can call down there tomorrow."

Tomorrow. The day before Albuquerque. I had work, my last lesson with Monty, practice with Arthur.

"I'll go down on my lunch break," I said.

I don't remember much more about that night. Maybe Buck had some words of wisdom for me, but they drifted right past me. I went to bed and lay there like a log. The moon kept me company for a while, then sank below the window.

I went to work next morning, and Buck had sense enough not to ask me if I was going to change my plans for the weekend.

When I called the detention center from the payphone in the locker room at Tomasita's, I had to make my way through a computer jungle before I met an actual voice. Then a woman told me my son was being processed. I wouldn't be able to see him till Sunday. She couldn't tell me anything else.

I drove by the detention center after work. I'd never seen it before. They build those places in the part of town most people never see, near the garbage dump and the warehouses. Gray, concrete, no windows. There was a prickly pear cactus near the door. It could have been a cannery.

I backed out of the lot and drove to the studio.

Monty put me through my paces, told me I was moving good. Maybe it wasn't a compliment, just a plain statement of fact. I beamed. Then Arthur came in, carrying his black Stetson and his boots. He put them on, wanted my opinion. I said they were just fine.

We went through our routine, and I told him what Monty'd told me: he was moving good. He was. Something liquid and lively in his long bones—the music and my leading called it out. Like he had an excuse to relax, finally, and just let it all flow.

After an hour, I said I was tired and went home.

Buck was standing at the kitchen counter, eating pizza. He'd saved two slices for me.

I went right on past. In the bedroom, I took my suitcase out of the closet and started packing for Duke City.

16

I wasn't prepared for the matched outfits I saw as soon as we walked in the hotel ballroom, but then I wasn't prepared for anything that went on that night at Fiesta.

The matching wasn't the kind I'd chosen; male and female were clearly marked out, aqua cowgirl shirts with fringe teamed up with aqua cowboy shirts with fringe. Of course the fringe on the his-and-her shirts hung a little differently on the women. It was the way people used to dress twins, too cute for words.

But as soon as I saw Arthur in his regulation black jeans, I knew we were in show business. Those jeans were brand-new, stiff, cut high, and if he'd been less of a gent he'd have complained about crotch rub. He did walk a little stiff, like he'd been thrown a day or two ago: the true Western style. That was fine by me.

My black jeans were new, too, cut high and tight,

and skinny as I am, it wasn't hard for me to master that horse-ruptured gait. So when we sauntered onto the dance floor, arm-in-arm, only a stickler would have noticed the swell beneath my white shirt. I had my orange hair tucked up under my hat.

The judges were sitting on a raised platform; two men and two women on our right, the same combination on our left. They looked like the judges I remembered from tobacco auctions in the Purchase. Pure Country, these judges, and serious, like they were going to recommend a hanging. They had green pens, poised at the ready, and score cards, and they were already marking things down.

"Dancers, take your positions," a woman in a split dress hollered. We lined up on the dance floor with two other couples. Arthur had pinned my number—186—on the back of my shirt, I'd pinned his on, and we were as ready as eight safety pins could make us.

All around the floor, people who looked like my relatives in the Purchase were sitting on folding chairs; it was the tobacco auctions, again, only these people weren't looking to make money off a cash crop. No drinking and no eating, just big jugs of water and paper cups on tables in the corner, and the lights were so bright the dance floor looked like a great big operating table. "Country's short on glamour," I told Arthur; he was squeezing my hand tight, and he gave me the kind of smile that showed he hadn't heard a word. I sniffed up the air, expecting the brown tang of cured tobacco, but all I could smell was electricity and whatever cleaning fluid they'd used on that floor.

I'd seen Monty across the room, with Lolly; he was warming her up. He had a raft of his best lady students lined up for the Pro-Am—he was going to be dancing every dance—and I guessed he had a lot on his mind though he didn't look it, laughing and joking with Lolly while he took her through the Rope Twist.

"He's still stepping on her toes," the sorrowful tune began, and I counted the beat to Arthur. He'd gone as stiff as a board. The eight judges' sixteen eyes were drilling into my back.

Then we moved out. After about thirty seconds, Arthur loosened up, and we started our routine.

Judges don't like to call things to a halt once they're started, even when they have every right to do it; they want things to move right along, keep to the printed schedule. Cattle judges, tobacco judges, dance judges, they're all alike, that way. I saw one whisper something to another, but she shook her head, and I figured that was the end of their worrying about me, for the time being, at least.

My leading was just a touch of the hand, a nudge of the thigh, the way I leaned back into his arm—nothing anybody could see, unless they were looking real close. Which of course those judges were. But who can gauge a woman's touch on a man's shoulder? Who can measure that little pressure of the thigh? One of them would have to have been plastered between us like a sheet of paper, to feel it. That's how good we were—him, catching on so fast, me, barely touching him. It was what I'd always thought leading should feel like—light as the graze of a butterfly's wing, but doing the job.

We only had a minute and a half to show our stuff, and then that doleful tune was over, and we were facing the judges. We hadn't rehearsed that part, but we took our little bow like we had—both of us ducking our heads. The other women were dropping curtseys, holding out their skirts, and I thought, Thank God, not me. There was some light clapping, and then we walked off the floor. Those judges were still staring.

Standing at the edge of the floor, waiting for our next round, I had a chance to size up the competition. Right away, I started feeling good. Sure, most of those people had been dancing Country since they were out of their cradles, but I didn't see a lot of polish or dash. There was a couple from the Four Corners area who had a pretty special Swing routine, fast and jazzy, but she was dressed in sequins and I didn't think the judges would go for that. We were supposed to look Country, Country and family, both. Then there was a group of four from San Diego who were into some fancier footwork than I'd seen, but so what? Fancy isn't everything.

After a few minutes I went to get a cup of water and then I sat down next to Arthur to wait.

He said something that surprised me: "I'm just in this for fun, but you have an ax to grind, don't you, Mel?"

It wasn't really a question, so I just gaped at him.

"I don't mind," he went on. "It's just something I noticed."

"Your history shows on your face, like the song says."

"Guess so."

"It's not much of an ax. It's just the way I feel, always have felt. Leading comes naturally to me, and I never have had a chance."

"So be it. I just hope we can enjoy dancing without worrying too much about what happens."

"How come?" He knew—I didn't need to tell him—how bad I wanted to win.

"Because look." There on the floor was a couple I hadn't noticed before, little tiny people, whirling around so fast I could hardly see them. Each step was exact and fine, like they'd been practicing for years. Pretty—both of them pretty, I thought, like those plastic couples on cakes.

"They're good," Arthur said.

"They're not in Newcomer."

"Still . . ."

"We're pretty good, too."

"Mel, we've been practicing for less than two weeks."

I saw then he was fixing to lose. "Come on, Arthur—don't sing the blues this early in the game."

"Just want you to be ready."

"I never in my life have been ready to fail."

That fixed him. He stared at me like I was one of those strange women you hear about who really do think they can do anything—rock climb, have babies, run businesses, make millions. I never have been that kind of fool, but I know what happens when I put my heart into something.

Then the woman in the split dress hollered our number. This time, it was East Coast Swing. God, how smooth we started, how we flowed on that big floor, faces shining around us like little stars in a dark sky. Then I stopped seeing and hearing; I couldn't tell you what the song was. It was all just moving—touch, response, turn. I felt like I knew Arthur's bones, and he knew mine. Words didn't matter, or time spent together. Just touch, respond, turn.

Ordinarily I don't go for men who won't fight me, on the dance floor or off. They don't interest me. But with Arthur, it didn't feel like a question of fighting or not fighting. His shoulder was high and firm under my right hand, and his left hand felt as big and ridged as a catalpa leaf, but between those two fixed points, the man was liquid. Pure, shining melted gold. It flowed and flowed—energy, love, I couldn't tell the difference. Didn't want to.

The folks on the sidelines, all those little twinkling stars, seemed to be watching us now, following every move, the way a bunch of mothers watch their kids play. And I thought, This is it, this is heaven: to move, to be watched, admired.

I remembered that sign Monty runs on the electronic board at the back of the studio, little red lights blinking out YOU MADE US PROUD, and for about a second I wondered why nobody ever says that to me, and then I didn't care. It was being said now. I was saying it to myself. YOU MAKE ME PROUD—no red lights, but that didn't matter.

Then I noticed those judges still staring. One of them looked like I was hurting her eyes, and another was writing something down on her scorecard, shaking her head like a grade school teacher writing out a note for me to take home.

"They're onto us," Arthur said.

"It may be." I sounded calm, but I didn't feel that way.

I looked around for Monty. He was standing on the other side of the room, the side reserved for instructors and their students, but when he caught my eye he came right over. He had little Annie on his arm, a flower in a genuine cowgirl outfit. She was sweet-enough looking but fierce underneath, I knew, like a dried red chili.

Monty told us, "They're going to try to disqualify you." I could tell right away he was mad enough to fight.

Sure enough—the music stopped, and those eight judges went into a huddle in front of one of the green tables.

"Let them try," I said. The sight of all those backs turned against me made me want to kick like a cob. Monty grabbed my arm and squeezed it, hard.

I went to get some water, parting the crowd that was gathered thick around the edges of the dance floor. When I came back, I noticed the way Arthur was sitting, his arm around the back of the chair he was saving for me, and I knew he was going to feel just as bad as me—maybe worse—if this thing went to pieces.

Monty was talking to the judges now, both hands in the air.

The competition swept right on, in waves, groups of dancers taking the floor and going through their routines. Arthur and I had finished, so all we had to do was sit and wait.

I watched Monty on the other side of the room, working his way through the numbers with his chosen dancers, and all of a sudden I missed his sure touch. I wondered for the first time why I was messing with Nature's Order—what I'd heard somebody call the usual way of dancing. I'd never worried much, before, about the whys or wherefores, but feeling what Arthur and me were facing—being disqualified, not winning even a Bronze—and watching Annie and Lolly and the others, all my friends, women I truly liked and admired, taking their turns in the regular way with Monty, I wondered what it would be like to really want that—long for it: to be led. And all of a sudden I knew I was going to be living alone.

Buck leaving, for good—fed up. Me making the best of it. Sixty staring me in the face.

That's what thinking about failing'll do for you.

I shut those thoughts off, fast. They're catching, and I didn't want Arthur to get infected.

"It's okay," I told him. "Monty put in a good word for us."

Arthur said, "I'm trying not to care but somehow or another I do."

By eleven PM everybody had taken his or her turn and all the couples were standing or sitting around the room, waiting for the floor show to begin. Before that, though, the judges were going to call out the prizes: Gold, the best, Silver, next down the line, and at the bottom, Bronze.

I told Arthur, "The only kind of prize that matters is one they're not giving out tonight." It was a try, but he just shook his head, not looking at me.

And I thought about Buddy—all his missed prizes, the ones I hadn't given him and nobody else had, either—till this girl. It seemed to me she was going to save his life.

"Here we go," Arthur said when the judges stood up, and he took hold of my hand.

I let it lie there; it'd been quite a while since a man had done that. Married men don't hold their wives' hands, as a rule.

The judges had gathered up their charts and such and were climbing back up to their seats on the platforms. The head honcho had hold of the microphone.

He started with the Bronzes. A lot of people looked pleased as they flocked over to pick up their certificates, and I thought about all the walls they'd hang on, all the drawers they'd be stuffed in, to show the grandkids, one day.

When I heard my name, I shot up. Arthur was right behind me. We ran out on the floor, then stood hand-in-hand facing the judges.

A Bronze for Two-Step. Another for Swing. Nothing for Cha-Cha, that'd felt so good. Not the best, of course, but good for the first time out. I could hear our friends from the studio clapping and shouting.

I pulled off my hat and bowed, and all that orangey hair fell down to my shoulders.

There was a sound in the room like wind through trees. Before that sound could grow into a roar, I stepped forward, taking Arthur with me.

The judges were standing around the microphone, all turned our way. They were staring the way cattle stare at a strange dog that's come into their pasture.

I held out my hand for my certificate.

"Now I know which is which," the head honcho said with a big grin. "I couldn't for the life of me tell till you took off that hat."

"Well, you can tell now," I said, still holding my hand out.

"Ladies all wear skirts in this competition," a woman judge put in. She had a voice like a woodpecker working its way up a tree. "Next year we're going to write that in the rules."

"Never had a call to, before," another woman judge said. "Everybody just knew."

Monty was behind us now. "This is their first competition," he said.

I was still holding out my hand. They had those certificates, and I was bound and determined to get mine.

Then Monty pushed forward, and I saw those judges look at him like maybe he could be trouble. "They've registered and paid their money, just like everybody else," he said.

Then he was shaking hands with the judges and smiling like it'd all been some kind of fairly pleasant misunderstanding, but the certificates were still on the table. One of the judges had said they'd have to talk to the adjudicators.

"I don't care," I said, and I meant it. The dancing had felt so good.

That was all I needed, not papers with words written on them. Words belonged to a different language. I had what I felt.

"Don't you dare be disappointed," I said to Arthur.

He grinned at me. "Our first time, and it was fun."

— ~ — 17 — ~ —

I stayed on that night though it meant paying more than I could afford.

I could claim Arthur changed my mind, and the truth is he did ask me to stay; he had no call to hit I-25 at midnight with the drunks going back to Santa Fe from the Duke City bars. I told him I'd think about it.

Buck was expecting me, but when I called, I got the machine. It was nearly one AM, he was either asleep or gone, so I left a message with my room number at the Desert Inn, thinking he'd call in the morning.

When I went out to the parking lot to tell Arthur I was staying—he'd asked me to let him know—I saw a light come up in his face that was more than I expected and a lot more than I wanted.

"Good," he said, reaching out an arm to hook me into a hug, and I took a step back and said, "We better talk."

The twenty-four hour coffee place around the corner was empty except for a truck driver studying the bottom of his mug and a waitress who tried to sell us eggs—for the road, she said, like we were going to be hitting it together.

I ordered real coffee and Arthur ordered decaf, and just for a minute I missed the days when it would have been a trip to a downtown bar and another drink for both of us.

"All I want is to dance with you," I said before he could get started. "I told you that."

"I never asked . . ."

But I'd seen his face. "Sorry, Arthur," I told him. "It seems like I'm still in love with the ornery son of a bitch I married ten years ago, and the only other man in the world who means a thing to me is my son."

"I wasn't counting on anything," he said, choked up now with hurt pride. "I'm just surprised you decided to stay over."

Like most men, he knew how to cut his losses, fast.

"Well, the truth is my husband's probably out catting around somewhere and my son's been hauled back down to Texas to jail, so there's not much reason for me to hurry home."

"What'd he do, to get sent to jail?"

He didn't seem surprised, and I guessed things like jail had been pretty much run of the mill, at one time if not now.

"Broke probation," I said. "He used to be an addict, old charges piled up."

Arthur shook his head. "They're picking up the wrong guys. I was in law enforcement before I retired. The war on drugs—it's like Vietnam." He stirred a heaping spoonful of sugar into his decaf and I was glad he was still eating sweets. "We can't win—we're fighting our own kids, and we're too damn stubborn to admit it."

"More body bags," I said.

"Well, jail cells, anyway. Private prisons are one of the fastest growth industries we've got. They're not any worse than the other kind, there's just more of them. Looks like it could go on forever, as long as they keep turning a profit. Where's your son at?"

"I don't know. He's been in and out of trouble for years."

"I raised two boys, myself."

Here it goes, I thought, wishing now I'd ordered eggs and bacon. I was low on strength for a late night sob story. When did men start sharing their troubles? They used to be so tight-lipped; it'd be years before the new girlfriend heard about the wife gone, the kids in trouble. I think all this truth-telling must be something we taught them.

But Arthur stopped there. He made me think of Buck, sitting on his past like a big brown broody hen on a clutch of eggs. It was a relief, though, at least with Arthur. I was pretty sure it'd be the same old story: wife run off, or run off from, kids raised anyhow.

"I guess we all have our stories, by this time of life," I said, to put a period to it.

He wouldn't let it go at that, and I got the miserable feeling my dancing partner was hooked through the gills by his past. "Your husband's a lucky man," he told me, like I was the last one to know it. "How come he doesn't dance with you?"

"Says he has two left feet."

"There's plenty at the studio can hardly walk a straight line."

"He'd never let me lead."

Arthur looked down at his hands, cradling the coffee cup. They were nice hands, wide and strong-looking, with big flat nails. "To tell you the truth, I don't like it much, myself."

"You didn't say that at the start."

"It took me a while to get up the nerve."

"Why'd you let me do it, if you feel that way?"

"So I could hold you in my arms."

I'd led right into that.

He looked up at me then, and I swear everything I love about men was in his face: courage, and generosity, and the straight-out flash a man gives you when you're what he wants. At least, right then.

And why the hell, I thought, should it last? It's now, this minute, that counts, not some time next year I can't even imagine. That was left from my girlhood—the faith I never have been able to stamp all the way out in doing what the moment calls for.

"Thank you," I said, looking him in the eyes—blue, that flash still there, though fading. "This is all there is to it, Arthur, for you and me both." Tough words to say, but I more or less meant them.

"Well, I guess we're straight on it now," he said. "I ought to thank you for telling me the way things stand."

"I guess it's a half-hearted thanks."

"That's the truth." He was smiling. "Most ladies I know wait till the next morning to tell you."

"Eat their cake and have it. I've never gone for that."

Arthur asked the waitress for the check. I guessed from his sideways glance at me he hadn't given up, maybe never would give up all the way, which was fine by me. Talk about eat your cake. I didn't want him looking at me dead-eyed, the way men do when they know you really are out of bounds.

"Tell me about your boy," he said, raring up to dig his wallet out of his back pocket.

"There isn't much to tell. Crack got him after I chased him out of the house. It was either him, or my new husband—one of them had to go." I'd thought it often but never given it words. Words made it stick.

"You blame yourself?" he asked, laying out money.

"I'm not looking for comfort, if that's what you mean," I said. I know that route. Even the customers try it. "Don't your feet hurt?" they ask me. "If they do, I sit down," I tell them, "and not on your lap." I can make my own comfort, pay for it, too, if need be.

Then we stood up to go; the night was being reeled in around us. Truck traffic would go on till dawn, heavy on the throughway a hundred yards away, heading down to El Paso or up to the Colorado border.

Through the coffee shop windows, the Sandia Mountains looked black against misty city lights. There's no such thing as darkness, now, even in the desert. Walking out, I felt the dead loneliness of that time, that place.

Arthur put his hand on my waist.

"Dancing is dancing," I said, moving off. "I like it more than just about anything in the world, but it's a dancing partner I want, nothing more. Let's take some workshops in the morning. That's the reason I'm staying over, I want to learn some more of those fancy turns."

I left him standing by the boom of that all-night road.

18

Buck didn't call me in the morning. When I telephoned home, the line was busy. So he was there, but hadn't seen fit to track me down. I couldn't wait around to try him later; the first workshop, in Country Waltz, was starting at nine AM.

I called Arthur—he sounded like I woke him up—and told him to meet me out front. Then I put on my practice skirt and my red boots and did something about my face and hair.

Ten minutes later I saw Arthur standing half asleep in the lobby next to a bunch of fake white tulips. "Wake up," I said. "I want to learn the Rope Twist."

He did.

We went on from one workshop to another, Country Waltz to Beginner Two-Step; by the end of the morning, I was satisfied we knew as much as we needed.

Changing partners around the circle, I met guys

from Phoenix, Denver, Ship Rock. They all looked like they might be more comfortable someplace else but they were trying hard, and I wondered who for. Get ready for that thang called love: a girl friend or even a wife who wanted, bad, to dance, and would find some other partner if the one she had didn't agree to learn.

There was something else beyond all that hard trying, though, and it was what I was looking for: not love, at least not the man-woman kind. I don't know how to put it into words without sounding corny. It had to do with joy, the church kind I used to get when I looked at the sun shining through the stained glass windows in that little church in the Purchase.

And something else, too: those feet pounding the dirt at the pueblo dance—that connection. Who we are. Who we've always been.

At noon I went back to the Desert Inn to pack my suitcase. The red message light on the phone was flashing. Call home ASAP, the operator told me, sounding like I ought to know why I was needed.

By then I didn't want to call. I wanted to go back to the coffee shop and have a grilled cheese sandwich with Arthur, and laugh. We'd danced well together all morning; we were moving beyond that time when two bodies are just trying to get used to each other. I hadn't been sure he'd still let me lead, but he sank back into it just as natural.

We were getting close to knowing how to move together by feel alone, like in the dark when you know where the chair is, and the table, without reaching out your hand. I'd had that with Buck, no doubt about it, and I think he'd had it with me, most of the time, in bed; for us, knowing by touch was our main way of getting along.

With Arthur, getting along didn't matter; we weren't ever going to have a joint checking account, or argue about who ran up what bills, or try to figure out what to eat at night with nothing in the house. It was just the pure joy of touch and moving together—all I thought then I'd ever want.

The message light burned all that out of me. I called home, and

Buck answered on the first ring. "They've taken Buddy on down to El Paso."

"I thought maybe they'd have a hearing first."

"I guess they did, some time yesterday—I don't know. Anyway when I called down to the jail a while ago, they said he was gone. A couple of deputies drove him down. Probably handcuffed in the back of the parole car."

That was all I needed to hear. A picture of Buddy formed in my mind, and I knew what I had to do. "I'm driving down there now."

"Come on home first and I'll go with you."

Buck doesn't usually offer, and I knew he was trying to make up for lost time, but I had a fire in me to get moving and I knew I had to be moving south. The mother in me had woke up with a snarl.

I told him it didn't make sense for me to drive all the way back to Santa Fe, and he didn't say anything more, no goodbye, just hung up, fast.

I threw my clothes in my suitcase, paid my bill, and headed south on the throughway, glad for the light Saturday morning traffic. My head cleared out, and so did my life.

An hour south of the city, I remembered I didn't say goodbye to Arthur. I was glad. I didn't want to explain.

So it was all foolishness before this, I thought. All time wasting, and staving off old age. I looked at my face in the rearview mirror, and I swear I didn't recognize myself. Who was that woman all cracked up with wrinkles? When did I get that old? I didn't know, couldn't tell. I felt like I'd lost myself, buying red boots and dance outfits I couldn't afford while my son was in and out of jail.

Whatever lesson my body, growing old, was trying to teach me was a lesson I hadn't wanted to learn, but now it seemed like I knew it already, in my bones: giving up, giving over, those fires just about put out. Was it time passing, or disappointment with life that'd made it easy for me to say no to Arthur, easier and easier to say no to Buck?

Younger, I did anything, which was why I had Buddy. I didn't like to think I hadn't planned him, but there it was. Being me as I was at that time with Paul meant neither one of us did any planning. And so Buddy "came along"—as my mother said; she saw the truth of it the one time she visited, coming all that way from Kentucky by bus. You still could, in those days; they'd put you down at any crossroads.

I remembered her in her white raincoat with her big umbrella and her heavy suitcase—she had no notion what to expect, in terms of weather, but she figured that and everything else out pretty fast.

I'd cleaned the shack on the edge of town where we were living—temporarily, of course, till something better turned up—, cut and hemmed curtains, even tried to bake bread. The loaf turned out an inch high, heavy as concrete, but I sliced it and Mama ate it like it was good. She'd brought me two jars of her homemade sour cherry jam, lugging them all the way across the country.

She thanked me for the bread, and then she took another look around the shack; I'd shown her the pallet bed I'd made up for me and Paul so she could have the real bed in the corner.

"I believe I saw me a motel a ways back towards town," she said, and that was the end of it; I drove her right on over. I thought for a long time it was the buckled particle board walls and the plug-in heater with the frayed cord in that shack, but it wasn't. She waited till her death bed to tell me: she wanted her privacy.

Maybe that was when I stopped believing in believing, or stopped believing. It's the same thing, in the end. Her putting up with me was love, maybe, but it wasn't faith.

Feed my sheep, the Man said: all I'd been able to hang onto, as the years passed. Feeding and being fed: but what did old age do, even to that? The rations thinned down as our poor old bodies aged till there was nothing left to give or receive.

All that time I was driving south like a fiend, the pickup bucking. By late afternoon I was halfway down to El Paso. Things were flattening out and the fields looked as brown as Indiana, nothing much growing, and the little towns leftover, run down. It was hot, too, and the glare reflected off the truck's hood.

There was a steady stream of traffic, heading someplace, and I wondered how many of the people in those cars and trucks were heading for prisons or hospitals, clammed up in silence, like me. There wasn't a thing on the radio that seemed right and nobody in the world I wanted to talk to.

I stopped at a roadside shed that called itself The Hamburger Place, with all kinds of paint decoration around the "the": across the road was another hamburger place and likely as not they'd been fighting each other for customers for years.

Really it was a bar, with food on the side. In back was a big room dark as a tomb, hung with antlers; the juke box was the only thing alive back there, and it was humming and flashing in that self-satisfied way jukes have.

There was a plastic rose in a vase on top of the toilet tank in the bathroom, which led me to believe a woman was involved although the only people up front were two ranchers in cowboy hats and an old boy behind the bar, swabbing at it.

I put on lipstick and tried to blot out the old-lady face I was seeing in the mirror, and sure enough when I came out the two hats were staring at me and one of them wanted to strike up a conversation.

He told me how this was the town "Mr. Hilton that started all the hotels" was born in; he'd given the school a whole bunch of computers to show his appreciation.

"For what?" I asked him.

His knotty old leathery face looked surprised. "Why," he told me, "for growing up in a decent place where everybody knew everybody and said hello on the street."

I nodded and ordered a hamburger, medium. It tasted pretty good, not one of those flat frozen patties but a real hunk of ground meat.

The bartender came over then and told me he was the owner, and he wanted me to know the place across the road was going broke fast. He thought it was the poor quality meat they used. There'd been enough tourists, going east to the wildlife sanctuary, to keep both places in business, at least for the summer, but winter was going to be a different matter.

Then he said, "We give all the pretty gals that come in here something to take home and think about," and he handed me a business card.

"Turn it over," he said, and when I did, I saw PERMIT written in black letters across the top, and some words beneath. "Here, I'll read it to you," he said, seeing I was so slow on the draw, and he took the card and read in a voice everybody in there could tune in on:

"'This certifies that I . . .'" (He left a blank there and winked at me) "'legally wedded wife of'" (another blank, another wink), "'do hereby permit my husband to go where he pleases, when he pleases, and drink what he pleases . . .

"'And further, I permit him to keep and enjoy the company of any lady or ladies he sees fit, as I know him to be a good judge. I want him to enjoy life in this world as I know he will be a long time dead.'

"Here's the place to sign," he said.

"How come it says, 'Void unless countersigned'?" I asked.

"Well, we figure it takes two to tango. Both of you's got to agree to it for it to stick."

I started to feel in my purse for a pen.

"You going to sign it? Nobody ever signs it right off the bat, that I heard of."

"I'll wait," I said, thinking I didn't want to sign it with a boot, and I put it in my purse.

"You got somebody to give it to?" the bartender asked, looking like he'd bitten off more than he could chew.

I showed him the picture of Buck I keep in my wallet.

"Whewee," he said. "That man of yours is going to be tickled pink."

"If I sign it," I said.

Then I got up and went out.

Back in the truck, I buckled up and drove on. Along the way, I started thinking about Buddy, the baby and the little boy, both long gone. I had a picture of him around age two in my wallet that it would never occur to me to show anybody.

Maybe I never had really known him, even at the beginning, when they laid him on my stomach in the delivery room. I knew where he'd come from, well enough, and how—that pain's too bad ever to forget—but I couldn't tell who he was, even then, screaming and throwing his legs around, then stopping, staring, shaking all over.

He scared me—that's the truth of it. Nothing of Paul and nothing of me seemed to be in him. They said he was cold, and took him and wrapped him up, and after that I didn't see him for a whole day; that was the way they used to do things, and I grieved like something gone crazy. Grieved, then went numb and slept.

When they finally brought him back so he could nurse that thin yellow stuff that's supposed to be full of all kinds of goodness, I wanted to ask him, "Who are you? Can you tell me?"—him snorting and pulling at my nipple, wild to eat, to live, and then strangling on the little he got and going purple.

Everybody else thought I knew who he was; I'd made him, hadn't I?—with a little help from Paul, who looked at him fish-eyed from the doorway and asked, "Doesn't he ever stop crying?"

"Sure he does, when he's had enough," I said, trying to be the expert, but I didn't know.

Well, there it was. I didn't know who my son was, even at the beginning, and I was afraid to ask. I was still afraid to ask him, all these years later: Who are you?

Did I find out, later on? Well, some. There were days when he was three—after I stole him from Paul—when he'd be mashing a black crayon across a page in a coloring book, and I'd think, Yes, he's me—only maybe a little bit wilder. But then his face would draw up in one of those terrible looks, and he'd ask me why I took him away from Taos, and where was his daddy?

He never did actually ask me. Asking would have been too easy. I'd thought out all kinds of answers: how Paul drank every Saturday night and lost hold of himself; how he'd take his belt off and threaten to "lam that kid" for next to no reason. I thought Buddy would remember those times and know I was just trying to save him.

But he never gave me the chance. He never asked.

Now and then I'd feel him watching me when I was putting on my waitress clothes and jabbering about how much he was going to like whatever baby-sitter I'd managed to round up. He'd give me that look, like he missed his daddy who used to watch him when I was working, packing him along in the pickup when he had an odd job to do or a friend to see. All that ended the dawn I snatched him up with an armload of clothes and left Paul snoring.

I tried to make it up to Buddy, tried too hard, bringing home any man who seemed halfway decent and setting him up with my son at the kitchen table for a home-cooked meal—fried chicken, cornbread, okra and tomatoes, lemon meringue pie, the meringue yea-high.

But Buddy wasn't buying it. He'd come to the table for the food—he was shooting up fast—but he only had a yes or a no answer to whatever questions the strange man put to him: school, sports, the usual, and after the pie, the kid would be off like lightning to TV or a pickup game in the trailer park.

And later—after Buddy was supposed to be asleep—the sex didn't make up for what I missed, and I wanted to ask each and every one of those men, "How come you can't be a daddy? Don't you know how, or don't you want to?"—never allowing that it might be Buddy that ran them off. Because they all left, and soon.

Then Buddy turned thirteen and the trouble started. It didn't come as any surprise. I didn't know exactly what to expect, never had, but trouble wasn't any stranger than anything else. Life was trouble, is trouble. Why should I get off scot-free? The only thing I didn't know was what shape or form his trouble was going to come in.

I never thought about drugs, even though Paul had been in the thick of all that in Taos, those years before people started dying or going to rehab. It seemed like drugs belonged to those times, that place—nothing I could call wrong, or sinful, to use Mama's word, because all the pot we smoked didn't do anybody any harm that I could see. I thought all that was just a part of being young, and Buddy never had seemed young, to me.

He started much earlier than we did, though, and it wasn't just pot. I knew that smell, would tease him about it. But then, over one summer, he dropped everything he liked: sports, most of his friends. He found a new bunch that hung out on the back side of town, near the library, where there's a dark old alley, with sheds and trash. The kids were hiding, now—from me, from everybody. I felt Buddy slipping away, but I didn't know what to do.

When I worried about him, I used to remember that old house in the Purchase, with the walnut tree by my bedroom window. I'd climbed down that tree many a night, bent on trouble, but I always climbed back up it again before dawn; I didn't think about missing breakfast, even if I'd been out till four AM. Something held. Something holds, even now.

The one time I was back there in recent years, I went to see that walnut tree.

Mama's old house has been all fixed up—aluminum siding, a screen porch—but the walnut still grows up against the side, brushing what used to be my window.

When I saw that tree, I felt like I did when I saw Mom and Pop's graves—just names and dates on granite. It was all right; it fit. Who cares about the frowning they did, or the criticizing? Their looks brought me back up that tree at four AM and down to breakfast at seven, no matter what I'd been up to in the night.

I'd done plenty of frowning and criticizing with Buddy but somehow the message never got across.

Driving into El Paso, I asked directions for the jail. It wasn't hard to find, in a seedy part of town next to the old rail yards.

I parked at the curb and went in: a slow, hot afternoon. The place was jammed—I expect it always is—mainly Hispanics, and a lot of babies and children, with white lawyers and social workers hurrying back and forth like bees.

Now and then somebody was pushed into one of the courtrooms that rimmed the big central area—a bull pen, with dirty sky lights. Now and then somebody came out and was hurried off somewhere, crying, or clutching a child, or looking defiant, or dazed.

Garbage was everywhere—soda cans, paper cups, cigarette butts, overflowing the bins, heaped on the floor. The line of people at the drink machine plodded along, fingering change, lit up by the greasy florescent light, and in the bathroom, a woman was penciling in her eyes and crying at the same time.

I'd gone to the bathroom to get a hold of myself. I didn't know what kind of trouble Buddy was in, didn't want to know. Now it looked like I was going to find out.

At the elevators there was a gun check and a woman in a uniform ran a clicking wand over me. I saw how everybody in the line knew how to stand, arms up, legs spread, and I wondered did we learn it from TV? I knew the drill, too. The clicking machine ran up and down and around and under, and then she nodded me through. Behind me, a girl with a handgun in her purse had to give it over.

I rode up in the elevator with four or five other people, silent, their shoulders hunched, facing forward.

The fifth floor was another big open area with beat-up metal chairs set around the walls. No windows. One wall had a smudged glass panel with people in uniform moving around behind it like fish in a bowl.

I took a chair. Didn't know what else to do.

A woman next to me was fighting with her four-year-old, trying to get him to sit down and be quiet. He wouldn't. On the other side, a preacher was reading his prayer book, mouthing the words.

Then a guard came out of the glassed-in room and called a list of names, and some of the people began to move toward him, slogging along like they were in deep water.

I went up to the guard and asked him what I needed to do to get on that list. He said to sign in.

I knocked on the glass panel, and a guard on the other side moved toward me, never looking up from some papers he held in his hands, and I thought how fish move, slow, in a big dirty glass bowl. He pushed a clipboard through a slot in the glass, and I filled it in: the usual questions. I passed it back, then lined up my driver's license with the others that had been left against the glass, so they could see if we were who we claimed to be.

And I thought, I've always lived decent. I wanted to say it out loud. Never had much, but always lived decent. What I meant was, no jail, before this. No jail, even with Paul. It matters.

I sat down to wait my turn.

The woman with the baby and the preacher had already gone in. A new bunch of people got off the elevator, went to the window, filled out the papers, lined up their driver's licenses, then sat in the chairs. I thought how this goes on, day in, day out, sun or shower, and how we must look to the guard fish, floating on the other side of the glass: losers, women mostly, chained to trouble.

I wanted to say, "I don't belong here." Probably each and every one of them wanted to say that, too.

Finally the guard called my name. I walked with my bunch of

people down a long narrow hall. That greasy florescent light was every-where, and the walls looked kicked.

We went in a big room divided by a table with a dozen chairs on each side. A panel of glass ran down the middle of the table, separating one side from the other.

We rushed to our chairs, and I remembered that game we played when we were little, running around a bunch of chairs that were never enough.

And then they let them in.

The prisoners.

Orange overalls, some kind of blue slip-on slippers.

I saw Buddy.

No hand cuffs. I tried to take some satisfaction from that—his long wrists free below the edges of those orange sleeves. I wanted to touch that orange, see if it was nylon, or what, like that would give me some clue about my son. Looking at his arms, I remembered when he started to grow hair there—I used to try to joke him about it.

I tried that again. "Never knew orange was your favorite color, Son."

He didn't say anything, just looked at me and sat down on the other side of the glass. It was smudged, smeared, from hands, lips. There was a little grate near the bottom for his voice to come through. He leaned toward that.

"I'm sorry, Mama."

"Don't sorry me." But tears came up and choked me. After a while I got hold of myself and asked him, "How come you never said that before?"

"Never felt like it, I guess."

I leaned close, trying to get a look at him. In those few days he'd lost weight; the bones in his face showed. His eyes looked paler, some-how. He was staring at me, one hand piled on top of the other on the ledge.

"How's my girl?" he asked. I had to think for a minute who he meant.

"I haven't heard from her."

"She didn't call you? I told her to."

Then he told me, kindly, like I needed the information I didn't have sense enough to ask for, "The baby's due in a month. Till I get out you have to see to her." He lifted one hand and dropped it, hard, on the ledge—a bit of the old Buddy. One of the guards standing around the walls started over.

"What's the problem here?"

I heard my son say he was sorry, again. Twice in five minutes—some kind of record.

"Keep it down," the guard warned him and went back to the wall.

"I'll take care of her," I said, "the best I can."

"Not good enough, Mom."

I didn't know what to say. "What're you charged with?" I asked him. "All they said in Santa Fe was they sent you back down here."

"Possession."

"That's all? And you got—"

"Forty-five days."

"You doing all right?"

He shrugged, warning me with his eyes not to go any further in that direction.

I sighed. "What can I do for you, Son?"

"I already told you. Do it, don't just try. I know you're trying. You quit halfway."

"That what you think I did with you?"

"Sure. Soon as Buck—"

"Eighteen years," I said. "Doesn't that count for something?"

"Don't give me that," he said. His tone had the guard looking.

"I'll pray for you."

"Okay, Mom."

"I will," I said, "every day—" trying to get him to say it mattered.

He smiled a little, then, like he was used to my trying things that didn't work and had quit holding it against me,

"What've you been up to?" he asked. "You and Buck?"

"Country dancing. Not Buck, though."

"I heard."

"I love it," I said. For a second, I thought I'd tell him the reason, straight through that smeared pane of glass. Then I got back my common sense. "I have my own way of doing it," I said.

"Yeah."

"That's not what I came here to talk about. I want to know"—I leaned toward him—"how you're going to manage."

"All right, I guess." He looked at his hands, stacked on the ledge. I saw the nails were chewed.

"You get to use the payphone?"

"Once a day for two minutes. I talk to Bridget. She's scared."

"Scared of what?"

"The baby coming."

I had to ask it. "It's yours, isn't it, Son?"

He gave me a black look.

"She seems like a nice girl," I added.

He nodded. "She wants to get married."

"What do you want, Son?"

He shrugged.

"It might be good for the baby," I said.

He stared at me.

"'Every child needs a daddy,' my mama used to say."

"Dad's been good to me, lately," Buddy said.

"I saw some of what he can do for you when we were at his home. Making up for lost time. Well, that's good—he owes you. Now he's married again—"

"I don't mean money, Mama."

"I didn't think you did." Our time was running out, and I needed to ask more questions. "How'd they get you?"

"Picked me up on the throughway outside Santa Fe for going eleven miles over the speed limit, checked their computer. I didn't have court permission to leave Texas."

"There you go," I said, "getting discouraged. Don't give up, Buddy."

"I'm not giving up." He shot me a stare that reminded me of Paul in his younger days, guarding his stash. Buddy leaned closer to the glass and whispered. "It's hell in here."

"Sure, it is," I said, to beat back the tears. "Has to be, so you'll mind your p's and q's when you get out."

He sat back, smiling, shaking his head.

Then the guards were coming toward us. One of them shouted, "Time!"

Buddy stood up with the others. I saw the line of them—twelve men in orange overalls. Twelve stories. The wrong road taken, then taken again. A little pot, some booze, a break-in—the usual. The anger, too—that room hummed like a hive of disturbed bees.

"What else can I do for you, Son?" I asked as he turned away. "Magazines? Cigarettes?"

He looked back over his shoulder. His face was stiff, now, blank, like all the others. A door opened into another room, bright as the inside of a refrigerator. The line of men shuffled toward it.

"See her," he said.

— 19 —

As soon as I got out of the jail, I called Buck and left him a message. I didn't know where I'd be staying in El Paso; I said I'd call as soon as I was settled. One thing for sure: I wasn't going to sleep another night under Paul's roof. I wanted to see Bridget alone.

Mrs. Lopez sounded sour when I called to tell her the family emergency was going to keep me away longer than I'd expected, but I figured I could sweet-talk her once I got back. Zozobra was coming up, and she was going to need me.

I didn't let Bridget know I was coming. I guess I wasn't sure how she'd take it.

When I stopped for a Coke and some gas, I hit the payphone with a handful of quarters. One of the things Buck and I never have gotten around to is a calling card.

I asked Paul's voice on his machine to let me

know how I could reach Bridget, and when I called back a while later, Paul himself told me sweet as cream she was staying in a little place they'd rented for her on the south side of town.

I wrote the directions in the margin of my map, already pretty well covered with hen scratches from all the road trips I'd taken with Buck, and for a minute it seemed like this was just another jaunt to Carlsbad Caverns or Ojo Caliente until I remembered Buddy's eyes and the way he said, "See her."

It looked to me like the neighborhood where they'd stowed Bridget was pretty much the twin of the one where Paul and his wife had put up their new house. This area was maybe a little older, with brick colonials and two-story frames from the fifties when some wise-ass developer first laid his eyes on that sorry piece of desert. There were gardens, and Mexicans handling shovels and hoses, but there was a patchy playground, too, with old-looking equipment and concrete benches, furniture for a neighborhood that never happened.

Everybody but the Mexicans was closed up inside their central air. A few of the larger homes had walls with broken glass on top and electronic gates; they were practically on the border, and they were taking precautions.

I parked in front of what looked like somebody's guest house—a friend of Bridget's mother's, I guessed—with a wooden arbor over the front door but no roses and two little windows like eyes.

She opened the door while I was still looking for the bell, and I figured she'd been watching for me. Her mother must have called to warn her, and I'd have given a pretty penny to know what that woman said.

Bridget had plumped up some even in the short time since I'd seen her. She was wearing a smocked pale-blue top and what looked like those old-time elastic-waisted clown pants.

"I guess maternity outfits haven't changed a whole lot," I told her as she stood aside to let me in. "I wore something like that with Buddy."

"Every time I see you, I wonder how come you're Buddy's mother," she said, leading me into a little room with two chairs and a table—the entire contents of somebody's attic.

I stood in front of one chair with my suitcase in my hand. I wasn't sure if I was welcome. "Why do you wonder?" I asked her.

She had her answer ready. "You look too young."

"Thanks, but I've earned every line and wrinkle. I'm kind of proud of my face. Road map of a hard life and all that. You going to ask me to sit down?"

That embarrassed her, and I saw she was still her mother's daughter, caring about people's feelings, about doing them right.

"Please," she said, with a try at a smile. "May I offer you a cup of something?"

"Thanks, but I had a Coke, a while back." I looked around the room: rose wallpaper, white curtains, and a sofa bed in the corner. Next to it was an old white wicker cradle. "Looks like you've got things ready."

"I didn't want to wait till the last minute." She sat down in the other chair and put her hands flat on her knees.

"When're you due?"

"Just under a month," she sighed. "You've seen Buddy?"

"Yes. He's doing all right." I started thinking how hard this must be for her, going through a first baby alone.

She sighed again, ducking her chin. "He calls me whenever he can."

"I know he wants bad to be here when that baby comes." I could believe in the baby now, almost see her, biding her time under that smocked top.

"He will be. The judge gave him forty-five days." She was trying to sound cheerful.

"Buddy was lucky to get off with that."

"He was set up." She jerked her head around and stared out the window.

"Listen, Bridget, Buddy's been in and out of trouble since he turned thirteen. He always claims he's been framed, but what happens to him is because of the way he acts." Then I was sorry. Bridget looked like the air had been let out of her.

"Well, he's clean now," she said. I felt for her, trying so hard to believe. She turned and looked at me, daring me to tell her something she didn't want to hear.

"Nobody kicks crack that quick," I said, feeling like I had to say the truth.

"I made it a condition," she told me, and I heard her mother's fine choice of words.

"Condition for what?"

"Being this baby's father." She laid her hand on the crest of her belly.

"I didn't know there was a question," I said, smiling.

"There isn't! But he's not going to have a hand in raising her if he goes back to using."

"Who's going to support you?" I asked.

"My parents, till I get back on my feet."

So Paul was winning this race, too. "How long you been calling Paul a parent?"

"He raised me," she said, sounding proud.

"He's come a long way," I said. "I guess I knew him in the slack part of his life. I used to have trouble rousing him out of bed."

"Since he married Mother . . ."

"She knows how to get him up and out?"

"Yes." She was proud of that. I guessed she came from a family of reformers. "She gave him back his self-respect."

That irked me. "Quite some present. What about my son's self-respect? You going to give that back to him?"

She was tight. "He's already got it."

"Best way to prove it, seems like to me, would be to support you and the kid. Act like the daddy you and he claim he is."

She shook her head. "Not until I know he's clean and has been that way for a year. I can't afford a relapse. This baby's not for sale," she added, patting her belly.

Money was weighing heavy on our talk, and I wondered what Paul had promised. It wasn't his money, but he wouldn't scruple to spend Emily's where it'd do the most good. "Buddy know about these conditions of yours?"

"There's only one," she said. "Yes. I told him."

I tried to feature it. "Over the telephone?"

"I wrote him a letter." I heard that weird little note of pride again, like it helped her to know how to do things. "Sent it to him the last time they picked him up."

So there'd been other times. I wasn't surprised. "He's an addict. It takes them a long time and a lot of support to change," I said. "I tried, for a long time, but in the end I just didn't have the gumption."

"He's not just an addict," she said.

I remembered when I used to say that. "No, he's a whole lot more than that, at least he was," I said, and tears came up in my eyes. I wiped them on the back of my hand. "I hate seeing the promise fade. His health'll go next."

"He swears to me—"

"He swore a lot of stuff to me, too." I felt tired all of a sudden, like we'd been having this talk for years and would go on having it the rest of our lives, and the craziest thing came into my mind: a picture I'd seen in a magazine of a church somewhere in France. I started thinking, I'll never go there, I'll never see that church. This, instead.

"He knows crack's ruining his life," Bridget was going on, with that drone I know so well. Addicts flatten out the people who love them, they start to sound like answering machines. "He doesn't even like to do the things he used to do—go out to eat, drive somewhere. All he does is sleep and wake up sweating and start pacing the floor."

"Pretty scary." My eyes were still streaming, and Bridget got up with a heave and fetched me a box of tissues. Taking it, I touched her hand. "Sometimes I wonder why we don't go to France instead, look at churches."

"Instead of what?"

"This."

She stared at me. "I couldn't just leave Buddy."

"I couldn't, either. Nobody can." I touched her hand again. He skin felt smooth, young. "You've got your work cut out for you."

"No. He has."

That was one lesson she'd learned, at least in words. "You've been going to meetings," I said.

"Mom made me, then I started going on my own."

I nodded. "I went for a while, till I got sick of all the sob stories."

"They're my friends," she said.

"Well, good. You're going to need them."

She settled herself in her chair again, sitting forward, her belly tipped toward her thighs. She was carrying low, another sign it was a girl.

"I think Sundance is kind of a weird name for a baby girl," I told her.

She smiled, and I thought she must have been pretty before Buddy happened to her. "Buddy chose it," she said.

"It's going to embarrass her to death, when she's older." I knew then I'd hoped they'd name her after me. I guess that kind of foolishness never dies. I decided to change my tack. "How'd you and Buddy meet?"

"At Paul's house—a potluck dinner in the back yard. Buddy told me it was his first solid meal that week."

I tried to imagine Emily arranging a potluck celebration for the return of the prodigal son. "How long ago was that?"

"Thirteen months," she said, like she'd counted every day. "I've more or less gotten my mind around the fact that my step-father's going to be my father-in-law."

"Paul and Emily will both help you," I said.

"I'm going to need your support, too," she told me.

I sat up straight.

"Buddy's my only son, this may well be my only grandchild. If you cut off Buddy, you cut off me."

She looked at me, straight as a ruler. "Buddy never has been treated fair," she said.

"I put up with enough. I put up with his father's drinking."

"Not for long."

"Two years. I gave Paul a lot of chances. You've got to give Buddy two years anyway, Bridget. Buddy never would've come looking for his dad if they hadn't had those first two years together."

"You think him coming here was a good thing?"

There was no use lying to this girl. "I don't know yet. It might be. I don't like to admit it, but with hindsight, Buddy might have been better off if I'd stayed in touch with Paul. You know what they say: a boy needs his father. I didn't want to believe that."

"What about a girl?"

"Same thing, I guess. Anyway, you can't cut Buddy out."

All of a sudden she was clouding up to cry. "I feel like I should, but I can't. I love him, Mel. Grandma," she added.

"Not yet." I stood up and put my arm around her. "I'm kind of looking forward to it, though." Not true, but close enough. I held her tight. "I'll help you any way I can."

She stopped crying then. "Thank you," she said, like I'd offered her a sip of cool water in the desert.

"You're welcome. Now I need to go."

I started on back to Santa Fe. It was late, and I was tired. I didn't want to spend any more money I couldn't afford on accommodations, so when I started to doze, somewhere south of Magdalena, I pulled the pickup into a rest stop and laid down on the seat. The picture of that French church floated into my mind, and I wondered why so much of

175

my life was taken up by other people.

But there it was. I needed my people, every one of them, even though they were practically crowding me out of my own life. I needed Buck, to tell all this to, and I got myself to halfway believe he'd be waiting for me when I drove back to the Wilderness.

He wasn't.

I washed up, poured out a bowl of cold cereal, made fresh coffee, and wrote Buddy a card to let him know I'd seen Bridget and she seemed fine.

The next day at work passed in a daze till time for my dance lesson. I was still beat, but nothing ever held me back from getting to the studio when I was expected. I put on my blacks and drove over for the practice party, where we all get to show each other what we've learned during the week.

I'd missed my regular lesson, and Monty was pissed with me. "You let everything get in the way, you're never going to improve," he told me, standing by the door watching his dancers circulate.

"I thought I already knew how to dance," I said, hoping to make him smile.

It wasn't that easy. "You know how to lead," he said. He said "lead" like it was a disease I needed to be cured of.

I didn't let that bother me. He'd been pissed before, and it always passed.

The best evenings of my life were those studio parties, when I whirled off with whoever was willing to let me lead—men, women, by then it didn't matter. It didn't matter much to them, either; I was weird, but that's nothing new, in Santa Fe. And I was a friendly weird, full of smiles because I was enjoying myself, and nobody can resist that. Besides, I'd learned to lead from the woman's position, so half the people I danced with didn't know what I was doing, and the other half seemed to feel like it was a relief. Who wants to always be the one responsible?

Monty watched me for a while, and he must have started thinking I looked pretty good, because he asked me if I could see my way to going to Vegas for a big dance competition coming up the next month. A group from the studio was going, and he thought it was time for me.

We were standing by the water fountain, where all the little used paper cups flock like sheep without a shepherd. "I'd never be able to afford it, even if I could get off work," I told him. "Mrs. Lopez is mad as a wet hen already, and Buck wouldn't favor it, I know. Besides, what about outfits? I've seen some of that kind of dancing on television, it's all sequins and feathers. Can you see me—"

I made the mistake of looking at him. He hadn't heard much of what I'd said; he was just waiting for me to slow down so he could tell me all the reasons I should go, which he did. And I listened, like I was caught on the point of a tin star. I wanted him to want me to go; that felt better than wanting to go myself.

Before I knew what I was saying, I'd told him I'd try.

"We'll stay two days, have a great time," he said. "You and I'll dance the Ballroom and the Latin numbers, too."

I asked him what it was going to cost, and it was pretty bad.

"Can I go as me, no feathers and sequins?" I asked.

"If you mean dress in black jeans and lead . . ."

"I do."

He looked at me, steady, now, and I thought how many women must have asked him to let them shine when they didn't know how to do it. "It's time to change that, Mel," he said. "This is a big Ballroom competition, they have a rule book a foot thick, judges from the top ranks of the pros. Here we accept just about anything, but in Vegas you'll have to dress like a woman, and you'll have to let me lead."

"Let me" set his mouth like lemon juice.

"You do, already," I told him, stalling. "Don't you know teaching is leading?"

He didn't fall for that. "I'm talking about technique, Mel. You back-lead here and nobody says a thing, a lot of your partners probably don't even know what you're doing. They'll spot that in a second, in Vegas."

"So what are they going to do, disqualify me?" When he didn't say anything, I pushed on. "Show me where it says in that rule book a woman can't lead."

"It doesn't say it anywhere," he said, and I knew he'd already checked. "But you won't win any prizes."

I thought about that. I'd seen the kind of prizes he was talking about—there was a shelf of them back in the glory hole: tall gold-colored figures of dancers perched on pedestals the colors of Christmas tree balls.

"I want to win," I said. "At least a beginner's prize."

I knew then I was going to have to take the bull by the horns. I asked him some more questions, acting like I was still making up my mind. But I didn't need any more information. I'd already decided.

The way Monty described it, I was going to do one dance alone, with him—a solo—and then a bunch of freestyles.

"A solo!" I said. "I never have done a solo in my life," and for some reason I flashed on the delivery room in that two-bit Taos hospital where Buddy was born. If that'd been my one chance to solo, I'd muffed it, and I felt the appetite rise to bite at that apple again.

"You'll do the American Rumba," Monty told me. "You're getting pretty good but you need to work on your Cuban Motion." That's the name for what we used to call the swing on your back porch. "I want to see you put your weight on the insides of your feet and rock through to the outsides," he said, showing me, his scuffed little black shoes precise as sparrows. "I'm going to enter you for Newcomer and maybe some Bronze."

All that sounded pretty big-time, to me.

I looked at the red electric beads, turned off now, on Monty's sign at the back of the studio. I knew what I wanted them to spell, and I wanted them to spell it for me: YOU MADE US PROUD.

I always had wanted big-time, at least a little piece of it. That was why I'd jumped at the talk show and all the trouble it brought—a tiny little bite of the big-time for a woman as common as dirt. Not the French church, maybe, but Vegas: my chance.

Driving home, I said outloud, "Mel, you've got your work cut out for you." And I didn't just mean dancing.

It was past eleven, and all the stop lights in town were on blink. Santa Fe closes down early, except for a couple of bars. I always know I'm in the right place when I see those lights on blink—something about being out later than anybody else, with the desert stretching on both sides all the way to the mountains.

When I walked into the Wilderness, Buck was watching TV in his underwear. I wasn't even surprised. He comes, he goes; it's been that way for years.

"How'd it go in El Paso?" he asked, tipping up a can of beer, his eyes on the screen.

"Fair to middling," I told him. "The girl's going to be all right. But she's talking about cutting Buddy out. I couldn't go along with that."

"You never have cared a horse's ass for family, Mel," he said. "Don't you think it's a little late to start now?"

"How do you know what I care about?"

He grinned at me—"Teapot!" I was standing with my hands on my hips; he always calls that teapot. "You care about having a good time," he said. "That much I know, for sure." He picked up an envelope. "The Visa bill came."

I didn't want to hear about it—my boots, the extra lessons, the outfit for Duke City. "Wait up a minute," I said. "What's wrong with me enjoying myself? I work damn hard to earn the money to pay my share of the bills."

He made a face like he was going to say something about my age or some such garbage. I didn't give him a chance.

"Isn't that what you're looking for when you light out of here?"

I asked him. I hadn't taken my hands off my hips. "You get yourself into places I don't even want to know about and blame it on me because I'm out dancing. I'd say we both share a liking for fun, only mine's aboveboard and cheaper."

He stood up, using his height, and I was glad he was in his stocking feet and didn't have the inch and a half his boot heels give him. "If you don't want to know where I go, how come you're always hinting about it?" He grinned that grin again and I wanted to smack him but knew better.

"Listen, Buck, I'm going to Vegas for a big competition," I told him, "and that's all."

"You do and I'm out of here," he said, easy as paint.

"You'll come running home with your tail between your legs, after a while."

"Not this time," he said, still so calm.

It'd gotten to the place where I depended on riling Buck, to where I kind of understood when some asshole hauled into court for beating up his wife could say, "Judge, she was asking for it." Halfway, I said. No woman deserves that. But I knew the pattern, plain as the Rumba: say something, say something fresh back, then either a smack or a slam out the door.

Either way, it always got fixed after a while, with him coming back and me saying I was sorry—even when I wasn't anywhere near to it. I wanted to keep him at home. Always had, thought I always would. This time, though, there wasn't any pattern, just Buck standing there in his stocking feet, defying me.

"Oh, you'll be back," I said.

"Just try me," he said, still easy, still smiling.

"Where you aim on going?"

He gave it to me then. I'd been wanting to know for a long time, then not wanting to know. He'd kept it all for when it would do the most good.

The other woman—that I'd always suspected and gone my way, letting sleeping dogs lie. Now he gave her a name—Maria—and a house, just over the border. "I'm going down there, spend some real time with her like she's always asking."

I felt my heart drop like a stone. I said, "And you want me to quit dancing."

"That's different," he said. "A lot of men touching you—different men. Maria's the only one, for me—other than you." He said it like it made sense.

Now she had a name, I knew I'd never be able to forget her. It hurt me so much I had to go sit down.

"When I'm here, I'm all yours," Buck said, and I knew he'd thought it out on a lot of long jaunts south. "When I'm with her, I'm all hers." Yes, I had to hear that. "But now you're always gone, Mel, that's the truth of it."

I was still choking on my hurt. "You married to her? You can do that pretty easy, south of the border." And then I wondered why I had to make it worse.

He shook his head. "I'm married to you, Mel."

"How come you never told me—so I could go ahead and feel sorry?"

He'd turned his back, staring out the window over the sink. "You haven't been sorry for a long time."

I laughed then, I couldn't help it. An awful cackle. "Maybe I don't know how to feel sorry anymore. Anyway, what difference does sorry make?"

He shrugged, and I saw his wing bones rise under his cotton shirt.

It came to me then. "So that's what happened to our folding chairs."

I'd said ours. I didn't know if I'd ever say it again.

He nodded. "She wanted to go on a picnic."

In the old days I'd have beat on him with my fists, drumming on his back till he turned around and caught hold of my wrists. Now I just stared at his wing bones. "So that's where you'll go when I leave for Vegas."

"Go, and stay gone."

"She prepared for that?" I couldn't say her name.

"She's prepared for anything."

"She probably thinks you're going to help her cross the border, find her some honest work."

"I don't think so. She has family in Nogales. She's a family-type woman."

"You're speaking up for her." I tried to smile, but it came out a grin. "I don't believe I've ever heard you speak up for me."

"You don't need it, Mel."

"Like hell. Like fucking hell."

"What about all those men you dance with?"

"You think they speak up for me?" All of a sudden I was so tired I had to go lay down on the bed.

He came after me. "Quit this Vegas foolishness and we'll talk things over."

"So you can just go back to business as usual?"

"I haven't heard you complaining."

"Quit hanging over me. Sit down."

He sat in the chair with the broken arm. I'd never gotten around to having it fixed, and now I knew I never would.

"Face it, Mel," he said, and I thought how he'd never sat so close without touching me somewhere. "Me being gone never bothered you, till now. You always said you liked your space."

"Space! When did you start talking like that?" He didn't say anything, and I had to go on, "I didn't know what you were up to, before. I mean I didn't know the details. From now on I'll have to know, I'll have to see it."

He sighed. Then he leaned down and put his hand on my bare arm.

I pulled back. Didn't plan to—it was just like his hand burned me.

That did it. He stood up and left.

The spirit is willing, my mother used to say, but the flesh is weak.

All this because of the goddamned dancing, I thought, but I knew that was only a small part of the story.

I laid there and sobbed like a baby. It was true: from then on I'd have to see things in my mind—him putting his hand on her (Was she younger than me? Prettier?), him coming into her at night.

But the worst was those damn lawn chairs. The little things: sitting outside on a warm evening, drinking beer. Loading up to go someplace, with a bucket of fried chicken and beach towels. Setting up those chairs in that new place, side by side.

I started out that night the way I'd started out so many others, walking the floor, going over what we'd said in my mind again and again.

Then, some time toward midnight, I just gave up. A fresh breeze was coming through the window over the sink, stirring my curtains, and I thought of that wind brushing the long miles of desert below the mountain range I could just barely see in the thick summer darkness. It seemed like nothing mattered except that breeze, and I let it take me back to the bed and lay me down.

I slept that night the way I used to sleep in the Purchase, with the climbing tree brushing its leaves against my window. There're no trees to speak of in the trailer park, but I swear I heard leaves moving in the wind all that long summer night.

20

Next morning Mrs. Lopez was waiting for me at the front desk. I knew right away when I saw her face I ought to expect the worst. And sure enough, she did it: fired me.

"It's Zozobra," I said. "You'll be jammed."

"I can't count on you, anyway. Likely as not, you'd be gone."

"It's just the last few weeks. Don't ten years count for something?"

She shrugged, and I thought, Shrugging is what life's giving me right now: people who don't even need to bother to answer.

She was already on her way to do something else.

When I walked to the locker room, it seemed like everybody was looking the other way. I knew how talk flew around Rita's; me getting fired wouldn't come as any kind of surprise.

While I was getting my things, Nancy Sanchez walked over and asked me if I'd told Mrs. Lopez I expected two weeks' notice or else severance pay. Nancy was all the time looking out for our rights, as she called them, and I couldn't help smiling at her. Then I just shook my head, and she turned on her heel, disgusted. What she didn't understand is that for once I didn't have money on my mind. I had my life, or something close to it, taking up all my mental space—my life, and what had happened to it, at least partly because of my dancing.

On my way to the door, a few people patted at me or said something, but I didn't see or hear. I'd stuffed my things into a paper bag somebody handed me, and I just went on out. One of the cooks, Ernie, I think it was, shouted something after me—Good Luck, or Have a Nice Day. I'll never know.

I've got other plans, I told myself, walking to the pickup, glad it was paid up in full and had a tank of gas. Yes, indeed—I have other plans. What they were, I didn't know.

First things first: I drove to the cash machine at De Vargas Mall and drew out all there was in our account—seventeen dollars.

Monty wanted his money in two days, to send in for the Las Vegas trip. I didn't know how but I knew I was going to get it.

I drove around town, something I hadn't done in years. Who has the time? Out toward Fort Marcy, the Lions or JC's or whatever were working on their giant figure of Zozobra, Old Man Gloom, getting ready for the party at dusk. I stopped to watch them.

They already had his body finished—about forty feet tall, plywood covered with painted material to look like an old-fashioned suit, long dangling arms and a big head like a pumpkin. They were trying to figure out now to hide the man who's the voice of Gloom—it's always the same man, every year—inside that body. Every now and then his voice would boom out over the loud speaker system, baying like a dog trapped in a hollow tree. It got me to laughing.

That helped. When everything falls apart, what else is there?

I never had thought what was done in the world was done just for me—who would be crazy enough?—but all of a sudden it seemed like they were getting ready to burn Gloom on purpose to get him out of my way, and I thought, okay. Thanks.

So I hung around town, went to a movie in the afternoon—in broad daylight! It was about a woman teaching college, living with her mother and trying to find a man. Same old same old, only with different trimmings.

Then I used my credit card on things I knew I was going to need—toothpaste, a change of clothes—and checked in at the El Rey Inn on Cerrillos. Got their last room. People were piling in for Zozobra, everybody's Albuquerque aunt and cousin; it's that kind of holiday.

I called Monty's machine at the studio and scheduled extra lessons without figuring out how I was going to pay, and after that I took a nap. I woke up dreaming I was flying over the Sangres, and when I saw where I was, I dropped right out of the sky, remembering the one other time I'd stayed at the El Rey, with Buck.

It was maybe ten years ago, when we'd been fighting and needed to start fresh. Without saying a word to Buck, I'd made the reservation and packed my little bag with bubble bath and the black nightgown Buck gave me for Valentine's. We hadn't had sex in more than a month and I thought it was Buddy, sleeping on a cot in the kitchenette.

It worked. I planned it to work. Afterwards Buck said to me, "I guess from now on we'll have to make it a special occasion."

I looked at him. He was busy buckling his belt. "Not too many special occasions in an ordinary year," I said.

"No." It didn't seem to faze him.

"What're you saying, Buck? We can't make love at home?"

"You're tired a lot and so am I."

"That never stopped us before."

He just shook his head.

"Maybe you don't feel private enough," I said.

"You don't make all that much noise." He was trying to joke me.

"Buddy sleeps ten feet away."

"I knew from the start he was going to be with us, you never made any bones about that—"

"No place else to go—"

"I know that, Mel. It's just the old peas in a jar story."

"What peas?"

"Something like, if you put one pea in a jar for each time you have sex before you're married, and then you take one out for each time . . . I don't remember exactly how it goes, but the point is, it goes down."

"Not this quick. Remember, we've both got plenty of grounds for comparison."

"That's for sure."

"One thing I liked about you from the start, Buck: you don't try to cheat me out of my past, and I do you the same favor. And you know as well as I do—"

"Well, it's not Buddy," he said.

I didn't believe him. I thought he was being nice, maybe even trying to act like the dad Buddy never had.

"It's got to change," I said. And I meant it. What I had with Buck was too precious to let go of.

A week later Buddy came home at three AM, waking us both. I heard his old clunker grinding up, scattering gravel, and I went to the door.

"I won't put up with this," I told him.

He stood down below me on the space of gravel where we'd put out the lawn chairs, and all of a sudden I thought, "It's summer, the child ought to be in camp"—my mother's voice inside my head. But he was too old for camp, filthy dirty, his face smeared with something that looked like vomit, bare feet big as claws on my clean gravel path. I knew now he'd looked something like that when he showed up with Bridget: worn down but hoping.

"What have you got to say for yourself?" I asked him, halfway wishing it'd be something I could take for an excuse, but he just stared at me. I saw then how blank and big his eyes had gotten, like the whites had been stretched by whatever he'd seen and done that night, and I said, "Cat's got your tongue," and reached to hug him, dirty as he was.

He stepped out of the way.

"I know you're getting ready to tell me to go," he said. "I've known it ever since you married Buck."

"That's not the reason—"

"Yes, it is," he said. "You've known him how long is it? Six months?"

"Nine," I said, like it would make a difference.

"Whichever. He's running your life now and I'm gone," he said, and went and climbed in that clunker and drove out of there, scattering more gravel.

I wrung my hands. I never had done that before. It came back to me like my mother's voice: hand over hand, my tough old knuckles grinding into my palms.

Later, when I told Buck, he said, "I don't know what call you had to do that," and I hit him hard as I could across his back, then nursed the side of my hand in my mouth.

"He'll come home," Buck said, not feeling my blow any more than he would have a fly landing on his shoulder, and he reached to put his arms around me, but Buddy never did come home, or call or write us a line.

I told myself as the years passed I had my old age to think about. I had my loneliness and what it would mean, if Buck left me. Well, I didn't actually think about that then, and it didn't do much good later.

Things changed afterwards with Buck. After that first time, he never did question what I'd done—I give him credit for that. "He's your son," was all he'd say. "Maybe it's time he learned a lesson or two in the school of hard knocks—" the only school Buck had ever known.

But after that it seemed like there was a shadow between us, and I think I know now what it was: Buck must have thought, deep down, that a woman who'll run off her own son will do just about anything to a man.

Not to be trusted, in bed or out.

I've always dreaded that.

What ended my wild days in Taos was knowing I was getting what my poor dear mother would have called a Reputation. It wasn't the petty stuff—grabbing a handful of tangerines, cashing a few bad checks. It was the in and out of various beds. That'll do it, every time. I took Buddy out of there and I took myself out of there while I still believed I could be trusted.

Remembering that made the bed in the El Rey feel like hot coals, and I got up and turned on the TV. But the thoughts kept right on parading, old thoughts I'd reviewed a thousand times in the past nine years: Buddy wanted to drink, drug, lay around, eat up my food—why should I put up with that? Time for the boy to stand on his own two feet, get a job, face the world.

When you act cruel to somebody you love, why do you claim it's for his own good?

Maybe it all boiled down to I'd been a mother too long.

Well, here I go, I thought: the long road back to blaming myself. I'd stayed off it as long as I could, trying to believe—still believing, somewhere—that the world and the Man had more to do with what happened in my life than anything I could do.

I felt pretty draggled-tailed, so I took a shower and put on my new blue jeans and pink shirt. It seemed strange not to be aiming over to Rita's, worrying about being late, and I wondered if Mrs. Lopez had already found somebody to take my place, then remembered that experienced waitresses are a dime a dozen in Santa Fe. Everybody waits tables sooner or later here, to pay the rent.

I'd been good at it, that much I knew, but what did it matter?

A smile, a quickness, riding smooth over dropped plates, bad tempers, delays. The truth is anyone grown up can learn to wait tables, till their feet give out. The tough part is getting to be grown up, but Mrs. Lopez never gave that a thought, because my growing up happened long before she interviewed me for the job.

I wondered if Buddy would find his own way to grownup-ness now, through the baby, and I remembered he'd given me my start on that road when he was only a little over three years old. (Not counting what he did for me just by getting himself born—that was the first lesson, and one of the hardest.)

I'd left Paul by that time, taking Buddy and an armload of clothes over to a room above the Adobe Sunrise, an old bar in Taos that's got a new name now and maybe a new reputation.

Back then the room up above was being rented to a friend of mine, and she was off somewhere and gave me the key. So that child and I moved into her rubbish—cut-out stars hanging from the ceiling, scarf-shaded lamps, incense in heavy waves, and some kind of a Buddha sitting in the corner—all that above the rowdiest bar in Taos, which is saying something.

What happened next (and I did this, not the world, not the Man) was I stayed out all night with a guy I'd met at the Sunrise, and when I finally came home about five AM there was Buddy standing in the middle of the floor in soaking wet pajamas, holding onto his teddy bear.

I got down on my knees, trying to explain—all lies—because there were tear scabs on his cheeks and his chest was still shuddering from a long bout of sobbing. I was crying too by the time I picked him up and changed him and put him back in the fold-out bed we were supposed to share.

Enough of all that, I told myself now; we all make mistakes—and I layered on the make-up and teased my funny orange hair and started out for Zozobra like I had no past at all. At least, that was what I looked like: dressed up and on the look-out. But the dull heavy feeling in my stomach wouldn't leave me, and I started to wonder if it ever would.

I always have loved crowds, noise—they carry you away. And there was plenty of both, heading for the big field below Fort Marcy, where they'd put up the figure of Old Man Gloom. Everybody was streaming down the Paseo in cars or on foot, converging at the pink temple on Washington Street, then wedging up the road. I was lucky to find a space to park the pickup behind the bank, a few blocks away from the field.

It was coming on to dark, which is when they fire up Gloom, so I decided to climb the Hill of the Martyrs to get a better view.

There was less of a crowd on the hill—most of the people were down below, in the field—and I could see Zozobra, lighted with search-lights, his long arms commencing to wave and that voice that was like the croak of doom itself coming out of his grinding mouth.

Mariachis were playing in the field, couples were dancing, and somebody was shouting over a loudspeaker, but above it all, Gloom's groans were rising and his waving hands were begging and pleading: Don't fire me up, don't kill me off.

People around me were drinking beer and aiming binoculars, and one kid climbed right up on the big white cross that honors the priests the Indians murdered in their long-ago rebellion, and I thought, All right. It was an Indian kid.

I remembered the long-haired Indian kid in Taos more than twenty-five years ago who'd ridden me away from the Adobe Sunrise on the back of his motorcycle, away from my son, my duty—my heart—and figured this might be his son, grown and drunk, sitting on top of the Cross of the Martyrs. The years fold into each other the way they always have and always will, and there's some satisfaction in knowing we all went on one way or another from the moment I saw Buddy standing soaked with his teddy bear in the middle of the floor.

The past was still catching at me like a briar I couldn't brush off, so I accepted a beer from the guy standing next to me and then started shouting along with the other people on our hill:

"Burn him!"

Burn the past along with him, burn all that pain and guilt, let us wake up tomorrow morning like it's the first morning of our lives and everything—everything!—is still possible.

Then the first puff of smoke poured out of old Gloom's forehead and his eyes lit up, bright green and rolling, and his long arms reached up and his fingers clawed at the flames in his white hair. The huge crowd below us in the field began to scream and all of us on the hill joined in:

"Burn him! Burn him!"

I remembered the crowd shouting when Pontius Pilate asked if they wanted him to free Jesus or Barabas—

"Barabas! Barabas!"

—and I wondered if the crowd all those years ago thought they were going to kill off the sadness of their pasts along with the innocent man they'd named King of the Jews.

Now flames were shooting high out of Zozobra's head and the mariachis were going wild, almost drowning out his groans, and I thought of that old man folded up inside Zozobra, groaning into a microphone till his voice gave out, and all the time, "Burn him! Burn him!" from every direction. I thought for sure they think they're burning up their past, and I'll throw mine in, too, a twig on that bonfire.

I was ready to, and pay the price.

After a while I got tired of the noise and the crowd and went back to the pickup and a long night at the El Rey, tossing, wondering why I was doing what I knew I had to do. I did figure out, though, how I was going to pay for it.

Next day at my lesson when Monty told me I'd have to give him a check for the Vegas trip, I knew exactly what to do: I asked him if he'd take cash—"Legal tender," I told him.

He said he'd take whatever I had to give, with his practiced wink, and corny as it was—all Monty's ways of flirting were corny—it lifted up my heart.

I went directly back to the Wilderness. When I unlocked the door, the emptiness smelled of garbage nobody'd taken out (I wasn't going to, that's for sure). I went to the little drawer under the bathroom sink.

I half-expected what I'd stored there to be gone—I didn't know, anymore, what Buck felt he had a right to—but there it was in its cracked leather case, the diamond necklace and earrings that was all I had or ever would have from my grandmother Randolf in Virginia.

Mama left the set to me in her will, along with a couple of other things that've gotten lost, stolen or pawned along the way. I'd held onto the necklace and earrings all those years because they were my only connection to what my mother called "Expectations": the old southern way that doesn't depend for its charm on money but on something harder to come by and harder to describe.

Class, those ladies might have called it.

I took the set right on down to the pawn shop on Second Street. The old guy there fetched his loupe and then went to the back room for a while, and I thought, Good, because neither of those things had happened when I'd brought in Buddy's jam box after he left, or the fancy radio Buck bought me one Christmas, or even my mother's pearl studs.

Then he came back and looked at me out of the corner of one pale eye, and I told him right off the set wasn't hot, it was all I had from my grandmother.

"How come you want to get rid of it?" he asked, like he took a personal interest.

"I don't want to get rid of it, but there's something I want more than holding onto it," I said. "I never have worn it a day in my life"—and we both got a chuckle out of the thought of me, the way I was dressed, the life I certainly looked like I lived, wearing the diamond set my grandmother wore when she was led through whatever that old-time dance was the girls used to do in Richmond.

He offered me three thousand dollars, cash, which was just over what I needed for Vegas, and I took it gladly and drove right on out to the studio and put the envelop in Monty's hot hand.

"That's goodbye to the only claim to a decent past I've ever had," I told him. He didn't get it and I didn't care. Randolf and Virginia were like tin buckets now, full of stale water, and I was throwing them, buckets and all, down the deep well I believed was my future.

Caroline took time to tell me she had some costumes I could borrow—we're about the same size—and I guessed she knew if Monty didn't what that money meant; women are quick, that way. I started to tell her about throwing the buckets of stale water down the well, but then I thought, So what? Who has to know, except me?

So it was set.

And finally I was free—cut loose from the feeling I used to like quite a lot that I was secretly different (Randolf, Virginia) from the general riffraff I'd been spending my life with; which included Buck, I thought, but never Buddy. Buddy had to be special, like me.

Lying awake that night in the El Rey, I knew I wasn't sad anymore, might never be sad again, and the empty Wilderness meant just that: a tin-can home Buck and I had vacated for our own good if separate reasons. The past had no more claim on me than that stinking Wilderness. All of it was gone, burned.

Vegas—Dreamland—was coming up, and beyond that I didn't want to see.

21

The garden of Caesar's Palace is a parking lot. His statue guards it, sitting on a big stone horse. Other places I've been are just what they are; Vegas is also somewhere else. All history is here.

Caesar's cannons gush water alongside the treadmill into his casino; the treadmill moved people into the casino as smoothly as coal cars going into western Kentucky mines. It's yellow inside the casino, chandelier light, and the green tables look like little grass plots, graveyard plots, well-kept. Shining, clicking, ringing machines are lined up row after row, with raised perches in front of each machine: bird stations, I thought, for the flock of birds gathered there.

Women were sitting on the perches; most of the men were at the tables. One woman was scooping coins out of a well on her machine while it clicked and rattled, pouring out more. One was sitting humped over a note she'd written to herself—a warning, or a recipe for winning?

A big man in red suspenders, his walker parked behind him, leaned into the green grass plot of one of the tables like he was looking for a four-leaf clover. Behind that table, a blond lady in some kind of uniform was palming cards.

I stood there staring at the white stubble on the back of that old man's head, wondering who trimmed his hair and why she went on doing it when he only wanted to bow down into that green pit, like he was fixing to pray.

An army of babies and old people in strollers and wheelchairs was being pushed along between the machines, all of them, old and young, blinking, and the ones pushing them looking far ahead, like hunters lost in some jungle.

Bells were jangling like Christmas gone crazy. After a while my ears smoothed out the jangling, and I thought, This is church music. We're closed in here together in this yellow light like candles', with the slots ringing and chiming.

Then I heard a guy shout, and a few people rushed over to his machine. He started scooping out coins like there was no tomorrow.

I walked outside, to breath the real air—the air in Caesar's has no smell or taste. Gas fumes and stale frying oil made the street seem real.

I didn't miss the others in our group, the seven who'd come from Santa Fe. They were getting settled in their rooms, but I can unpack a suitcase any time. I wanted out as soon as I got in.

I started down the strip, studying the row of hotels, thinking, Now I don't need Rome, or Egypt, or churches in France, or even to imagine, some dark night, that I've missed them.

Walking along in that crowd of wanderers, everyone stopping, gawking, pushing on toward the pink towers of the New York, New York hotel—and I could already see the big green arm of the Statue of Liberty, coming out behind it—I thought, Grandmother Randolf would be—what?—astonished, for sure. Her diamond necklace and earrings she never took out of the drawer were lying in the pawn shop in Santa Fe, and I was moving along here, thinking about a dream I'd never had.

Maybe she'd be proud of that, too.

Passing by a big bald stretch of ground behind a chain-link fence, I figured it was where they were starting to dig for a new hotel, and I remembered the old days when Buck used to take me sometimes to one of his sites—showing me off, I thought, though he never would admit it. He'd check on the electric going in or the way they were laying tile in one of five or six bathrooms, and I'd trail along behind, knowing those workers were eyeing me. Fine, by me, then and now. I liked to believe I did Buck proud.

I put my ten fingers through the chain link and hung on, looking in. Something was hurting me. I hung there like a shot crow till I could figure out what it was: it seemed pretty likely I'd never do Buck proud again, something I'd never paid much mind to and now missed like a chewed-off piece of my own heart.

On the other side of the fence, a man in a cowboy hat had parked the front part of his eighteen-wheeler and was letting his wife out of the sleeping compartment. They strolled over toward a parked American flag-painted helicopter that promised views of the Grand Canyon.

Another place I'd never thought of seeing. I wondered if there was a Grand Canyon hotel, further along.

Next I passed a man squatting against the fence, holding out his cap, a piece of cardboard perched on it. He turned it so I could read it better: "Hungry Need Help."

Never give money to beggars is one of my rules. I work, they can work, too. But this guy, squatting there, looked like a part of me torn off and gone adrift. I dropped a quarter in his cap, wished him luck.

"No Hiring on Site" the sign on the gate behind him read.

You'd think they'd want somebody to sweep, anyway.

Buck used to give a few hours' work on his construction sites to just about anybody who showed up and could walk. Said there was always something they could do.

Why didn't I remember that, those last months when we were hardly speaking?

After that I saw them all around me—the lame, the halt and the blind. Come here like everybody else out of hard need. One man with a stub arm shaped like a club held out a Styrofoam cup with his good hand; no message, this time, none needed. I put in a dollar bill. He grabbed my hand and kissed it. Next was a picture of a woman in a bikini with a paper bag over her head. "Come in," the sign said, "and see the unknown comic."

Stub arm. Hunger. Paper bag. Somehow all the same. Somehow all me.

If this is what traveling does, I'd best stay home, I thought.

Except it was too late.

I walked up to my room in the FloraDora (is that a place, somewhere like Florida?), all white, with pink flowers on the wall, and the big towers of a new hotel going up outside the window. I sat down to try to think, but the thoughts wouldn't come for the excitement.

It seemed like I ought to take pains, dressing up for our first dinner together as a group. I put on a black top I'd borrowed from Caroline and a really short black skirt with a red fringe, and I stuck my orange hair down with enough spray to choke a horse. Blue paint over my eyes, and a whole lot of what my mother called (she didn't like it) rouge. Pink lipstick laid on thick to make my hungry mouth look harmless. That was for the seven of us, strangers nearly, except for dancing, who'd tumbled onto the plane in Santa Fe:

Monty and Caroline, shuffling tickets, worrying about people's suitcases.

Bill D. from the college, retired some kind of professor, and his tall wife.

Two other dance instructors—little Helen I'm fond of, her long ponytail tied with a bright red ribbon, and her sweetie, tall lanky Ken.

And me.

I just said I didn't know them, but I knew their way of moving from all the hours we'd danced with and around each other in the studio. Probably I knew them as well as their own mothers did the day they were born, because everything that mattered was in the way they turned, skipped, glided or ground around the floor.

Monty had invited us to his suite for drinks before dinner, and when I went up there, I saw him for the first time in all his regalia:

white Navajo shirt with big sleeves and embroidery down the front, red and green—some kind of secret message, I thought, that people in his tribe could read. Under that he had on his black Latin britches, cut high and tight, and pert high-heeled dance boots.

If that outfit's allowed, I thought, they'll accept anything.

He was pouring drinks, and joking.

Caroline was standing beside him, looking a little pale, I thought.

The Mrs. Professor was on the far side of the room, and I headed in her direction.

Name of Rose. Smart as a whip. One of those women who make me proud I'm one.

"Trouble brewing," she told me, jerking her high shoulder toward Monty, who was sending Caroline on some errand she didn't want to do. "You know those Indians, the way they are with white women, scalp 'em or kiss 'em, it's all the same thing."

The professor came hurrying over from the other side of the room like he sensed his wife was off the beam. On the dance floor or off, he moves like a bear, weaving a little from the effort of standing on his hind legs, but coming on fast. Stumpy legs just flying and something like a glare on his fine furry face.

All he was offering us it turned out was two glasses of Monty's white wine.

Monty was watching me from over in the corner of the room. Well, a cat can look at a queen.

Then I remembered I'd told him once I wanted to dance more than anything in the world.

That gives a man a handle.

He came over, fast. The bear and his lady went off the way folks do when they find themselves in the path of a missile.

Monty told me he liked my get-up, and I wondered when a man who's in the business of pleasing women runs out of words.

"Just remember, this is Vegas, not Albuquerque," Monty said, showing his big white teeth under his mustache. "If I see you trying something..."

He trailed off. I wanted to know what he was planning to do.

"I'll follow the rules, at least the ones I know about," I said, feeling that left me a little room to maneuver.

He nodded. I could have hugged him for that; maybe it was his white teeth.

Then he looked like he'd forgotten what to say next.

"When's our first dance?" I asked, to fill the gap. Monty's always tight with information. My father was the same way, hoarding the map on road trips, holding it slanted so I couldn't see, from the back seat, which road he was lost on. My mother never even tried to look.

"The Rumba, 8:08 tonight," he said, not consulting any schedule to remember; that's the way I knew how much the whole thing meant to him—the entire weekend schedule for the seven of us was printed in his brain.

"What're you going to wear?" he asked.

"I've got a full skirt to go with this top I borrowed from Caroline. I hope that'll do."

"It will."

I'd already told him I couldn't spring for the official costumes, stretch dresses with slits to nowhere for Latin, and Ballroom gowns all sequins and marabou.

"You look fine," he said. "You'll have to do something about your hair for Ballroom, though."

"I've got plenty of spray." I was still holding my head up, but the truth was he'd hacked a piece out of my sail. Even Rose, the prof's wife, was decked out in blue satin and spangles, which wasn't really her cup of tea; and Caroline had on red satin cut up to her crotch.

"Slick your hair down and you'll be fine," he said. "You'll look fabulous."

"I bet you say that to all the girls."

The air around us rose like a cake in the oven. He laughed, and I thought how fine he looked in that shirt his great-grandfather might have worn, doing a different kind of dancing. "They let you wear wild Indian stuff, never say a word?"

He laughed again. "Wouldn't dare to, these days," he said. "They're already tied up in a lawsuit with two men who want to dance together."

"Times change," I said. "They might as well get used to it."

"Maybe not that far," he said, leaving me to wonder if he meant two men dancing together or a woman determined to lead.

Caroline had come back and was telling us it was time to go to dinner, and Monty went out the door with her on his arm.

The rest of us trooped after.

We walked over to the hotel they call Excalibur and wandered around for a long time, lost in a big basement-maze where there were skill games with the same people hawking them I remember from old-time traveling fairs in the Purchase. All the meaty-armed women and skinny, flat-eyed men had migrated from Kentucky to be born again in a basement in Vegas.

It turned out Monty had fixed a surprise for us: not just dinner, which I'd have welcomed heartily, but a show in the big ring at the root of that hotel.

I hadn't had a surprise fixed for me since the last time Buck remembered my birthday of his own sweet will, and that was some years back—mentioned occasions don't count.

Monty got us all settled in seats around that ring, and kids began slinging hash onto the plates in front of us.

When the knights came prancing in on their big high horses, flying flags and banging drums, I was out of my seat before anybody else, clapping my hands. The knights were boys, I saw when they passed close, boys with waist-length dyed-looking hair and no shirts on, just some kind of armor vest.

Rose told me later she thought I'd lost my mind, the way I was clapping and screaming when they started to run at each other with lances; I didn't even know till the professor told me that the lances were fixed to blow up like firecrackers, not really to shatter when the boys hit up against each other.

I don't know why, but it made me happy, too, when I looked down the row of seats and saw Monty and Caroline holding hands.

Then those boys and their horses stamped out of the ring and we were left to eat dried-up chicken and potatoes with our hands; this was all supposed to be the Middle Ages.

Rose gnawed on a thigh and said, "I don't know why I'm here, I like my own cooking better."

Later, in the lobby of the FloraDora, Rose asked me would I help her with her false eyelashes, and I barged right on into her room just as though the professor wasn't fussing with his tailcoat in the corner.

I'm not used to handling tiny things, and when I saw those two sets of lashes lying down in their plastic box, I nearly told Rose it was more than I could cope with.

But she needed me, and that did it. I dabbed on some of the special glue, caught hold of Rose's left eyelid, thin as a petal, and stretched it tight.

By the time Helen knocked on the door to tell us it was time,

I had Rose fixed, and that sweet little lady was looking at herself in the mirror like she was new risen from the grave. Helen was waiting to hustle me to my room to get dressed, and I was glad she was there when I looked at myself in the mirror. It seemed clear as day I had no business wearing a skirt that looked like a green satin tent and a leotard top that flattened out my best points.

Helen, bless her heart, got me to believe it was nothing but the too-hard light over the bathroom sink, and then she picked up the can of spray and did the business on my hair till it stood up like a rooster's comb. That same dusty orange, too.

"Hung for a lamb, hung for a sheep," I told her. She didn't get my meaning.

Then she used my lipstick to add six layers of color to my mouth. When she was done, I looked like one of the big fake lilies down in the lobby, standing stiff as swords.

Helen took me by the elbow, steering me to the elevator like I might fly off the wrong way up the shaft. Rose got on with us, too, and rode down holding hard onto the arm of her professor.

The ballroom looked like an auction barn, and I could just see tobacco farmers coming in to finger the hands.

There were a few chandeliers, and some gold trim up near the ceiling, which you'd never find in an auction barn in Kentucky.

I started to notice other people: large women and little men was my first impression. I thought most of the women looked old enough to know better—I know I did, too—and the men looked young enough to take whatever was offered.

One instructor was practicing with his student right behind me, saying, "No, no, no," the way you do to a naughty child. I don't know what she was doing wrong, but she was frowning and concentrating hard. I wished her the best, with all my heart. It seemed wonderful to me, still does, the way we always go on trying.

Monty still hadn't shown up. The rest of us settled at one of the tables, looking like a small flock of frightened birds, with Helen and Ken doing their best to make us feel better.

Ken danced with me and then with Rose and tried to get us to laugh, but I couldn't even muster a smile, and I saw Rose batting her lashes like they were full of frightened tears. The professor was so stiff inside his tailcoat Helen had to walk him around the room like one of those mechanical toys with a failing battery.

Dance music was blaring out of a big black loudspeaker next to our table, and a row of video cameras was lining up like cranes on one platform while the judges were settling themselves on another.

I needed my teacher, I didn't know till then how bad.

Waiting, tapping my foot, wondering if my rooster's comb was falling down the back of my head, I remembered my leading days and knew all at once that was what was missing. I never waited on the roof of La Fonda in the summer darkness or at Alegria on Friday nights for some man to come up and start me dancing. I just went and found a partner and started us both as soon as I felt the urge.

Here at long last came Monty pulling at his collar with one hand and yanking up his britches with the other, and I was sick to see he'd taken off his Indian shirt.

Caroline pinned on his number—201—and somehow jabbed him with one of the pins, and he jumped and jerked like a bridled horse but didn't say a word.

Then he held out his hand for me and reeled me, and it was time for us to begin to show what we could do.

I thought, Oh Lord, here it is—here is where I prove what I'm made out of, or don't.

I put my hand on Monty's shoulder, just above the seam the way he taught me, and I pressed down and out the way he'd taught me never to do—the way Arthur had put up with, but this was not Arthur.

My other hand gripped his like it was a pebble.

His arm behind my back went tight as the tin ring on a whiskey barrel, but my back was hard as a washboard and I leaned into his arm, daring him to try to move me.

He was staring over my shoulder, his face as blank as a plate.

The American Waltz—"These are a Few of my Favorite Things"—passed in a struggle, the kind you wake up from knotted like a fist. Monty didn't want the judges to notice our struggle—they'd taken up their positions, like weather vanes, at the corners of the floor, and were already making marks on their clipboards—so he couldn't risk leaning into me and throwing me off my balance, he couldn't try stepping on my toes. It seemed to me we looked light and easy as two balloons just touching, with that little electric crackle; but we were fighting hand to hand and chest to chest, both of us starting to breath hard.

That simple basic waltz had some speed to it, and we swung out together like a pair of doors, joined at the hinges, looking balanced; but Monty's hand and his shoulder and his heart were fighting me for control.

We were well-matched in height and weight so the struggle was pretty nearly equal.

The ninety seconds passed, and I was gasping.

One of the judges, a good-looking black-haired man, smiled at me as we left the floor, and I wondered, Did he notice? But if he had, why did he smile?

"Don't do that again," Monty said, and his hand closed like a vise on my arm.

I took a breath. "Where's it written the woman can't lead?"

"They'll disqualify you."

"You going to tell?"

We were five-year-olds now, glaring at each other.

After a minute he jerked away without answering me and went to get Rose; he was dancing Tango with her next, and I knew the way he'd melt her with the pressure of his arm.

Hernando's Hideaway. Oh yes. We were in it now.

I watching him bending Rose into the Corté and saw her smile with every dip, leg angled out and shoulder and head slanted down, but maybe her spine was made to bend and mine wasn't. Maybe what I'd lost and found again mattered more than if I pleased Monty—bad as I wanted to please him—or even if I won; and I was mad to win.

Caroline was sitting next to me, keeping track of the events on the program, and I asked her how we'd look, leaning a little on the "we"; I wanted to know if she'd noticed.

"Really good," she said. "You've improved a lot, especially considering all the lessons you've missed."

I started to explain about my son and his predicament but it didn't seem worth the effort.

Then I decided to push it a little further and I asked Ken the same question.

"Fabulous," he said, with his big bright smile.

Helen was nodding yes across the table.

If they hadn't noticed, it seemed likely we'd put it over on the judges, as well.

Helen got up a minute later to help me change my costume for Latin. In the ladies' bathroom everything was flecked with gold: fixtures, walls, even the light that came down in bits and pieces. Big women were hoisting their skirts, going into the stalls to pee, then jerking at hose or shoulder straps, staring at themselves in the mirrors with that hard-eyed look women get when they're judging their appearance. Nobody had time for a word or a smile.

Helen roughed up my hair with both hands and spread that coxcomb everywhere—you're suppose to look wild-headed, for Latin—and I squeezed myself into the little fringed skirt that barely covered my bottom, and then I was staring hard-eyed at myself in the mirror, too, knowing I was a stiffer judge of myself than anyone else could ever be.

Spray can in hand, Helen flew at me, and every hair was standing on end when I opened my eyes. Then she told me to lay on the lipstick—I did—and led me back to the ballroom past a florist and the door to a wedding chapel I hadn't even noticed, before.

My eyes were coming back after the blindness that is fear, and I knew now I was ready for anything.

They were calling out numbers for the Rumba when we came back in, and again Monty was nowhere to be seen, and I knew, lead or no lead, I'd be lost without him.

Helen told me to get up and stand in the line of dancers waiting to go on the floor, and I stood there feeling like I'd lost a limb.

Here Monty came at the last minute, tucking in his shirt, and it was the Indian shirt with the embroidery down the front and the big balloon sleeves, and I could have shouted, I was so glad to see it.

"Now we're both breaking the rules," I said.

"I can get away with this, for Latin." He still hadn't looked me in the face.

"Don't you want to win something," he said as we walked out on the floor. "Newcomer, or something. Don't you want to win like crazy." He couldn't afford to make them questions.

"Yes. I do. More than anything in my life." The truth, when it finally comes out, always sounds foolish.

"Then stop this, now."

We stepped into dance position, and the tasty beat of the Rumba began.

"I don't think anybody notices," I said as I put my weight onto his shoulder, and I swear he melted away under it the way we ladies are supposed to do.

And I knew then—maybe I'd always known it, only not so clear—that leading didn't matter, following didn't matter. They were just words. What mattered was the way we melted into each other, "moving as one," the way Monty always described it. I never had believed him before because I'd never felt it, not in bed with a man, not even all those times with Buck when I was trying to understand, to make things work.

All that was still just lead and follow, and some bucking, too. But this was different.

A smoothness, a silkiness, even. A trading back and forth: my strength, his strength, different but matched. Two voices riding the same tune. It lasted about thirty seconds.

I thought he'd decided to give up to make our dancing look better, but then I knew he was fighting me still, and I had to respect him for that—risking the judges noticing the gripped look on our faces.

I fought back till we were locked together like two tigers in a cage, every foot placement and shift of weight a new stratagem in the battle—to take the other one by surprise, move in on a weak spot, get just a hair's breadth ahead of the beat and win the advantage on that step; but then something changed.

Monty never gave up but he stopped fighting so hard. Maybe he knew now the judges were not going to notice, and maybe he knew, too, how much he wanted to win.

I moved into the open space he'd provided with energy and dash I didn't know belonged to me. That silkiness, that lightness, came back.

The Rumba is my best dance, and now I could put my heart into it, keeping the smoky beat going through every inch of my big strong body. My feet learned an arch they weren't born with, and my arms curved out in the open position like I'd spent years as a girl in dance class, and I was floating from the waist up like a petal hanging from a cobweb.

I only had to increase my touch by a hair to move Monty the way I wanted. He was still fighting me a little, and I knew the open work was a relief to him because then we were just joined by our hands. All those steps were allowed to be mine, to do what I wanted with, and I circled around him only lightly held.

When we passed our table, I heard everybody shouting and clapping, and Monty nearly smiled.

The same good-looking judge nodded at me as we went off, and

Monty saw that and didn't say another word.

Then I had to watch the others for a long time, which was hard on me. I wanted to take the floor again, go through every one of my routines—tell the judges it was my time, the time of my life: clear out the place for action! Instead I had to sit with a paper cup of lukewarm water in front of me and watch the professor and Rose do their bronze Tango, and I had to speak to myself the way you speak to a spoiled child so I wouldn't hold how good they were against them.

There were only two other couples on the floor, and the judges were circling like coyotes to get a good look at each of them. I saw Rose's face over the professor's shoulder on their first swing around the floor, and she looked frightened. The professor's tall black back was stiff as a smokestack and his head looked like it was propped on the rim of his hard white collar; from the way he held himself, something was wrong, although every step and turn they took was correct.

Caroline and Monty both leaned forward, and then the professor stopped dead in his tracks.

Monty made a move with his hand to start them up again, the way you'd jiggle the switch on a wind-up toy, and after four beats, the professor began to move his feet, Rose following right along. I knew she was whispering to encourage him, the way couples do in the dead of night.

The professor was walking through the Tango now, each step accurate enough but the rhythm gone, and I remembered what it's like to try to cut your losses. Rose was holding onto him like they were drowning together.

Then he stopped dead again. The other couples skirted around them.

The professor shook himself once like a dog coming in out of the rain and walked off the floor, Rose trailing behind him.

He went to stand against the wall, Rose alongside.

Monty and Caroline were already on their feet, rushing over, and

I knew for the first time how much they cared.

I'd have given a lot to know what Monty said to the professor—Caroline had her arms around Rose—but from where I was sitting, all I could do was watch the professor's face, for information. He was dead-white under the raw brand of shame—I had to look away. I've always looked away from shame, not because I care but because I can't afford to feel it. Shame is catching as the flu.

Then Caroline came back to our table, leading Rose by the hand, and I looked at their two hands, Caroline's neat and small with pink nail polish, Rose's hard-used. We all clucked and commiserated to let Rose know it could happen to any of us, we were all in this together. What is partnering, anyway, I wanted to ask, but some kind of terrible risk? Rose sat down, looking flushed and shrunk.

Then the professor came back with Monty. They weren't touching, but I knew Monty was pushing him along on a wave of his own confidence.

I had nothing to say, and I was ashamed of myself for being so damned afraid of catching shame.

The professor went straight to Rose and held out his hand, and I saw his long straight fingers tremble, once, like something had passed through them.

She stood up, turned her face to him and smiled.

Without a word, they walked back onto the dance floor, and everybody clapped like crazy.

The other two couples were finished but the judges were still in place, and the same Tango music began to blare out of the loudspeakers. Rose and the professor stood poised in dance position, and she was watching his face like she could see it coming—the terror, the shame—and ward it off somehow.

Then he started her with a move too delicate for me to see, and her little feet went fluttering across the floor. He moved tall and stiff and dark, a high-limbed tree.

Monty and Caroline leaned forward, urging them on with their eyes, and now the professor was turning a corner neatly, his shiny black shoes winking in all those lights. Rose I didn't notice anymore; she didn't stand out, as long as she was following, and even her aqua dress faded. The professor was fighting a secret war against fears we couldn't dream of—I saw it every time they passed: the brand on his keen white face.

"Halfway through," Monty said, and he reached over and clutched Caroline's hand.

Then it was over and done, the music died with a screech, and Rose and the professor came back to the table and the whole room was clapping.

The professor looked at Monty, who was smiling and praising him—he'd stood up, to clap him on the back—and I knew nothing Rose could say or do would ever equal Monty's praise, Monty's smile, because he was a man who'd seen that worse thing, shame, almost win out over another man, and seen it whipped, too.

Then they started to call out the winners for these first rounds, and Monty told us all to join the crowd that was standing in front of the judges like a herd of cows waiting for the barn door to open. I didn't want to go, didn't feel I had any place or right up there, but Monty just herded me along with his elbow.

They were calling out names and numbers, and I heard my name and felt Monty prod me in the ribs, and then I was standing in front of the judge who'd smiled and he was handing me a little round paper label with a number on it.

I got another one, a minute later. They were both ones.

"Good going," Monty said, sounding too surprised for my satisfaction, and then he praised the others. Everybody had a one or a two; the professor tucked his in his pocket before I could see what it was.

It was late now, and the video cranes were folding their legs and people were milling around the stands selling shoes and costumes, and those people were trying to close up, too, knowing nobody was going to buy at this late hour.

Monty and Caroline checked us off as we went by on our way to our rooms, telling us what time to be up and ready in the morning and where to meet.

I was glad to head for the elevators.

A crowd of people in their oldest clothes was waiting in the lobby, going to bed after a day in the casino, and they stared at us like we were flamingoes lighting down among pigeons.

Riding up, none of us had a word to say. It'd all been said and done, at least for now.

We said goodnight in the hall that stretched out as long as a throughway, slid the plastic squares that stood for keys into our identical doors, and when the green bead lit up, letting me know I could turn the knob, I knew I was on my own till morning. Each room probably was identical, the TV catty-cornered from the big bed, with a picture of some far-off place hanging over it, but what went on in those rooms between midnight and eight AM was anybody's guess and might even prove surprising.

I fell down on my bed without bothering to take off my clothes. Just had the strength to open my purse and look at those two round numbers. Feed my sheep, the Man said. We'd been well and fully fed.

22

I dreamed that night, a princess dream I never had when I was the right age—party gown, tiara, glass slipper, and the prince. He looked a little like the professor. I woke up feeling warm and soft. The green lights on the bedside clock spelled out three AM, and the room was full of grinding noise.

I got out of bed and went to the window. Down below in the light from a maze of work lamps, I saw a hive of people. A bulldozer was chewing away at the edge of a huge hole, and in the hole men in hard hats were picking and shoveling. At the top, the big green Statue of Liberty stood holding up her torch like she was trying to shed some light on the situation.

They had a tugboat similar to ones I saw years ago on the Ohio parked high and dry next to the hole, and I guessed they were in an all-fire hurry to finish the hole and fill it with water and float that tug.

I closed the window to keep out a little of the noise and went on back to bed, wondering how much overtime those men were making. Then I thought of the guy with the club arm squatting outside the construction fence. Probably those men down there digging had day jobs too, and families, and were trying to hold it all together on little money and no sleep.

I started right then to think about Buck. The truth is I'd hardly given him a thought since I left home, and now I couldn't get to the telephone fast enough.

He picked up on the third ring. His voice sounded sour as nighttime breath.

"Where are you?" he asked.

"Vegas. The dance trip." It seemed like a year since I'd told him I was going. "I just won two firsts."

"Well, think of that." It didn't sound as mean as he wanted it to. "When're you coming home?"

"I've got another day here."

"You going to dance some more?"

"I'm signed up for twenty more free styles. I'm doing good, Buck, better than I expected."

"Where're you staying?"

I told him and gave him the phone number before he asked.

"I heard from Bridget yesterday," he said.

My ears pricked up. "Yeah? How's she doing?"

"Okay, I guess. The baby's coming early."

I knew without him saying what that meant for me, and I felt like I was shrinking. All the hot air of pride and hope was squeezing out of me and I was going down, fast, like a poked balloon. "Who's going to be with her?"

I knew Buck was sitting in the dark on his side of our bed, wearing his jockeys and a shirt and a pair of socks, his belly hanging over his waistband. Shrugging, in the dark, not a word to say.

"Well, she's got her family. They'll help her, when the time comes," I said.

"Your first grandchild. Maybe your only one."

"How come you're in the Wilderness?" I asked. "You told me you were hitting the road."

"I came back for a few things."

Something in the way he said it quieted me. "They're digging a big hole right outside my window," I told him. "The noise woke me up." I wondered if I maybe might tell him my dream—the one about the princess.

"Nobody's saying you've got to raise this baby," Buck said, like he hadn't heard a word.

I sat down on the side of the bed and wrapped the thin blanket around me. "You want to hear about my dancing?"

"All right."

"I love it just about better than anything in this world," I said.

"I guess you like being held," he said after a minute, trying to sound like a friend.

"You ought to know. You're the first man who's been willing to hold me, after sex."

"Not just willing, Mel."

"It's the moving. The music. Maybe the winning—" and I thought of the two round paper numbers hidden like cut diamonds in the pocket of my purse.

"You counting on winning some more?" he asked.

"I already won, I just told you: two firsts. Nothing else in my life ever felt like this—not working, or cleaning house, or raising Buddy, or trying to take care of you."

He laughed, and I could smell the darkness in the Wilderness.

"I tried, Buck," I said, and now I was calm as he was. "But it didn't feel like music, or moving, and it didn't seem to call for a lot of skill."

I left a gap for him to tell me that's why I'd done such a poor job of it, but he didn't see the opportunity, or didn't want to take it.

"It's all those men you're dancing with," he growled.

We hung up then. It wasn't a bad call, all things considered; I've had a lot worse, talks with Buck that left me feeling like a piece of chewed meat. It wasn't going to be our last talk, either—I was pretty sure of that—and I was glad we'd have another chance.

The grinding was still going on, with a new clang in it, but I lay down on the bed and went right back to sleep.

Ken woke me up, calling on the phone to tell me to be down at the buffet by eight, dressed and ready to dance. I was in a hurry to get showered and dressed and made up—aqua eye shadow at seven in the morning! I looked at myself in the mirror and thought, There's no fool like an old fool, but then I decided I looked pretty good.

Standing in the line at the buffet, I remembered I hadn't even looked out the window to see the color of the sky.

The buffet cost $5.99 and went on night and day. The line I was in was shuffling up to a desk where a grim-looking woman took your money and waved you through to her sour sister, who showed you to your table. There were six or eight rooms full of tables, and each of them was supposed to make you think you were in some foreign country; they had things hanging on the wall that brought China or India to mind, if you had that kind of mind. Between the various rooms there were planters full of false ferns.

Our party took up two tables, in the China Room, and as soon as we sat down we were up again, heading toward a long low cave with steam tables. People milled like a bunch of ponies turned out to pasture, then found their way to stacks of trays and started to meander down the food tables, trying to see under the sneeze screens. Breakfast, lunch and dinner were all mixed up together, bacon next to breaded flounder, broccoli by ice cream.

Monty was ahead of me, heaping his plate, and I guessed he'd been hungry more than once, I mean really hungry, not just looking for-ward to his next meal.

What's the strong appeal of a starved man? I can't tell you. Maybe it's the fisted-up mouth Buddy had when he was just born—the one appetite that shows no sign of ever slowing down. I pick at my food. Most women do. But Monty was piling his plate with scrambled eggs and raw-red roast beef, candied yams, strawberry Jell-O and green chili peppers, and I loved watching him add a last spoonful of mashed pota-toes and gravy the way I used to love the frown on Buddy's face when I was nursing him. Mother's milk and dried steam-table food: it's the male appetite that connects them.

Monty flew back to our table, and I made a beeline through the loud early-morning gamblers and the grandmas who'd been at the machines all night; I wanted to sit next to him. I wanted to see him eat all that food. He chowed down seriously, no time for talk, just a little whoop of satisfaction now and then when he stopped to get his breath.

Rose and I struck up a conversation, to fill the gap. On the other side of the table, Caroline looked like she was coming down with some-thing. She had a piece of dry toast on her plate, nothing else, and she was cutting it up into tiny bites with the side of her fork.

All of a sudden, Monty looked at his watch and told us to step lively; it was time to get to the ballroom for the first rounds.

Rose and I hurried to the bathroom to put on more lipstick and check ourselves in the mirror. Then we ran out of there.

"What's wrong with Caroline?" I panted. We were racing past the door to the wedding chapel.

"They had a fight last night. Helen said Monty woke her up, yell-ing—" the teachers were all sharing one room, to save on expenses.

"They'll be all right once they start dancing," I said.

"Yes," Rose gasped, hitching up her skirt to free her legs to run faster. In the ballroom, Monty grabbed me like I was a can of peas on a conveyor belt. "Don't do it again," he said. "I'm warning you."

I felt cold from the top of my head to my toes.

Then we were facing each other on the dance floor, waiting for the music to start, and I couldn't help liking the way he'd placed himself, exactly, like he always did, no matter what was up. His small, soft black shoes were lined up just so, and his back and neck made one beautiful straight line in his tail coat, which stood out coal-black against the riot of ladies' colors, and what my mother would have called his linen was gleaming: a true professional, a born teacher. I tried to draw some comfort from that.

Then the music came screaming out of the loudspeakers, a waltz edgy as a Tango, and I took a step toward him, already floating on the beat, and he passed his arm around my waist and took hold of my hand. His hand is smaller than mine and I was used to holding it curled up inside my fingers like a captured mouse, but now I couldn't get my fingers around it. He had my hand crushed inside his palm.

I leaned into him—it was second nature, now—and nudged his thigh.

His arm tightened around my waist till I was pressed up against his chest. I arched back from him, and he tightened his grip on my hand till I winced. His nails were leaving marks.

Good for you, Monty, I thought, you've decided to fight it out, and I leaned all my weight on his shoulder and looked for an opening in the crowd of whirling dancers.

He let go of me and I nearly fell.

Then he stepped back, frowning, looking over my shoulder.

I held out my arms; we were going to get back into dance position and waltz off, fighting our own private war that nobody else could see.

He pivoted on his heel and walked off the dance floor.

As he went, he reached behind his back with one hand and scrabbled at the number pinned between his shoulder blades—the number I'd expected to see in my dreams.

I stood there with my arms hanging down by my sides, and the other couples whirled around me like confetti caught in a downdraft; I could hear the skid of their feet.

Monty went over to one of the judges and said something, and then a voice came over the loudspeaker, interrupting the music: "Scratch 201. 201, leave the floor."

I walked off in a daze. I kept seeing Monty's hand scrabbling at that number, the sign of his profession, his pride.

When I got back to our table, Caroline was on her knees in her chair, pinning his number back on, and Rose was getting up to do her Tango.

"I guess I'm not dancing anymore," I said to Helen when Monty and Rose were on the floor.

"You're not dancing with Monty," she said, not looking at me. "And there isn't anybody else."

I thought about asking, "What's wrong with Ken? He's a teacher, too—" but then I knew I couldn't do it. I sat there feeling like a heap of rags.

Why had I done it—spoiled my chances, embarrassed Monty? Because I had to.

That was all I could come up with, and I knew it was no excuse. But it was the truth: I had to, and the reasons why I had to didn't seem to matter.

"He warned you," Caroline told me later when I went down with her to buy snacks for the others; I was trying to be helpful.

"I never thought he'd walk off the floor and leave me standing there."

"Leave you—!" She glared at me, and the woman shoveling French fries into bags heard her tone and stared. "You ever stop to think what this means to him? Having to scratch a student?"

"Maybe I'm just unteachable," I said, trying to smile as I gathered up a handful of ketchup packets. "At least he could tell the judges that."

"They know better," Caroline said, and I smelled the sharp odor of an angry, overheated blond. "They saw you dancing last night, when you won those firsts. You have talent, Mel—anybody can see that. If Monty can't teach you, they'll think it's his fault."

"I'm stubborn as hell, that's all—not his fault in any way, shape or form."

She jerked away from me to pay for the fries. "I don't know what you're trying to prove, Mel, but you're causing us a lot of trouble. Monty had you signed up for nineteen more dances and now he doesn't have anybody to dance with, all those times. It hurts the studio. It hurts all of us."

"Why can't he dance with somebody else?" I asked, humble as an ant.

"Because that's not the way it works. He can't put somebody else in at the last minute."

I followed her back to the ballroom like a whipped dog, and after a while, like a whipped dog, I wanted to snap at somebody and get a little of my own back. But I couldn't do it. They wouldn't give me a chance. The whole group just turned its back on me.

So what had I proved?

Nothing, except I was a fool.

I sat there the rest of the day, getting up to run errands whenever they'd let me; Rose wanted a lipstick she'd left in her room, Ken needed aspirin for his headache. After a while they let me do more things for them, and I was grateful. Only Monty kept to the other side of the table and never looked once in my direction.

I went up to my room around three and took off the costume and put my jeans back on, and then I sat down on the edge of the bed and cried.

Later I wiped off my face—all that make-up stained the wash-cloth—and then I went back to the ballroom.

I watched the others dance for the rest of the afternoon, and after a while I started clapping for them. They were doing great, and I knew how hard they'd worked for it.

When it was time to hand out the prizes, the professor and Rose got five ones and seven twos and some threes and fours, and Helen and the professor got a top student-teacher award, and Monty and Caroline came in third and fourth in the professional category. I'd watched their Mambo like it was something I'd only expected to see in heaven—that smoothness, that happy way of supporting yet freeing each other, Caroline's rose-colored skirt riding up her beautiful slim thighs as she leaned backwards almost to the floor in a dip Monty supported with his knee.

Ken helped Rose paste her numbers on a wooden plaque, and Helen was doing the same for the professor, and Monty was off somewhere being congratulated, with Caroline, and I was sitting on the edge of it all, wondering why the fact that the professor had walked off the floor hadn't worked against him. But then, he'd gone back.

Monty told us to go upstairs and rest and come down at seven prompt for supper, and he still hadn't looked at me, and I didn't know whether I was included; but then I remembered the supper was part of the package I'd bought and paid for, and I thought, I'm going to eat the supper and enjoy it, too.

I looked at television for a while, then showered again and dressed and even put some make-up back on—not the whole regalia, though—and started down to the ballroom.

In the elevator, I saw Helen, and she took one look at my face and said, "Monty maybe would have let you go on, but one of the California teachers said something about you leading and then he didn't have any choice."

I thanked her for wanting me to know why it had happened, but it didn't make me feel a whole lot better.

Something changed when we sat down at our table. People were looking at me, speaking to me. I guess they knew how bad I felt.

A waiter slammed a plate of chicken and veggies in front of me, and the music started, and all those people who'd worked so hard all day stood up to dance some more, this time for fun.

They looked different, more pitiful, somehow, the big women in their neon dresses shrunk in the shoulders, bosoms flattening, stomachs hanging out, ankles swelling over their shoes, and I knew I looked the same: wanting something, stretching for it, knowing it was far out of reach—the dream that was only touched on by the little round numbers most people had pasted on their plaques.

This dream didn't have much to do with winning; it was more the way we imagined we looked, in the big mirrors—a flash of whirling color, a smile, a man's dark arm around a fattish back.

Monty came over after a while and picked up my hand and I said, "You can't dance with me, I've got on blue jeans," but he just led me right out onto the floor and we danced the fox trot. I was as limp in his arms as he could ever have wanted me to be, and I thought he'd asked me why I couldn't have danced that way in the competition.

"You planning to go on taking lessons?" he asked me, looking over my head to steer.

"No." I heard the tremble in my voice. "I can't afford it, and Buck never has liked it."

He sighed. I don't believe I'd ever heard Monty sigh before. "You could've gone places, Mel. Your age category'll thin out pretty soon—people in their sixties think they're too old. You could have started winning."

I touched my forehead to his shoulder. "How come you never told me that before?"

"I didn't think you'd stick with it. I was right. It would have taken you five, six years of hard work—"

"Don't, Monty."

"But with your attitude . . ." He glanced at me. "I thought I could change that."

"I don't think anybody can."

"Well," he said, "I guess you got what you came for."

We were heading back to the table, and I knew this might be my last chance. The floor show was coming next, and after that everybody would go to bed. "No, Monty," I said. "I didn't get what I came for."

"What did you want?" he asked.

"I wanted to dance my way and win."

"You got a little of that."

"More, if you'd stayed on the floor."

He pulled himself up, breathed in. "I couldn't let you go on leading, Mel."

"I know one of the teachers said something—"

"That's not the reason. It wouldn't be right to let you go on that way. I have a responsibility."

"What about what I want?"

"Sometimes a teacher can't let a student have what she wants."

"I just wanted to dance with you my way, I wanted the judges to decide (if they even noticed) whether or not it was all right. I wanted to go on till they shouted us off the floor."

He was hot now. "I have to go by the rules. I believe in them. This is my job, my life, not just some kind of a show-off game."

"It's not a show-off game for me, either," I said, and now we were locked eye to eye, standing between the tables. "I learned the steps, put on the make-up and the costume, but when it comes to the way I move, all the rules are off. You know that, you just won't admit it because you're thinking about other things—more students, more money, your reputation. I'm not thinking about any of that, and I never will, not because they don't matter but because dancing matters so much more."

"I was thinking about you," he said. "Not those other things."

"Then dance with me the way I want to."

"No."

For a minute we stood staring at each other, and then he turned around and headed toward the table where Caroline and the others were waiting, and I went the other way, to the door and the hall and the elevator and my room.

Sometimes the parade goes right on by you and you hear it pass, drums banging, trumpets braying, and you can't put your fingers in your ears or stay away from the window because there's only one parade. After it goes, there's litter left in the street, a paper cup lifted and tossed by the wind, but the color and the noise have passed and gone.

I sat on my bed. It was dark outside, and the fake skyscrapers of New York, New York were lit up, and the digging in the hole was commencing again in front of the Statue of Liberty, holding up her dead torch.

I started to wonder how come I'd always believed I could be free. How come I'd thought there was no price to pay, all those years of moving on and making do, working, raising Buddy, trying men. I thought liberty meant not much money and no furniture and a pickup with a full tank and the key in the ignition. But the truth is I never moved far from where I first set down, a cut-loose young woman in Taos; the horizon was never a barrier and the mountains didn't look like walls, and as long as I had a paycheck and a set of wheels, I could go anywhere and do anything: till I rammed up against a rule I couldn't break or live with, till I saw the back of Monty's head.

The clanging and the grinding were getting loud, and I wondered why I couldn't just go down there, grab a shovel and a hard hat, and dig: bend and lift, bend and lift till my hands were raw and my back ached and I crawled to my bed without a thought in my head and slept till the wake-up call and the taxi to the airport and the plane ride home.

I was a middle-aged woman—it came to me like a revelation—and I couldn't go down and dig, and so I just sat on the side of the bed in the dark, and the clanging and grinding went on.

Some time before midnight, I lay down on my back and dozed, and when the phone rang, I thought it was morning and time to leave, but it was still dark.

"I'm down in the lobby," Buck said.

One of the first things I did when I got home was give Buck that card from the hamburger place in Socorro. He took it and studied it like he didn't want to get too close.

"I'm going to sign it," I said, and I scrabbled up a pen from my purse and did the deed, not the boot but my name, in plain writing. "You've got to countersign for it to mean anything. At least that's what they told me."

"How come you signed it?"

"I want to let loose of you, Buck. Then maybe you'll be happy."

He grinned. "Aren't you afraid I'll run?"

"I'll take my chances," I said, and I meant it. "Anyway, I don't want to spend any more time and energy fighting you. Go where you want to go, Mexico or any place else you can get to and get back from in a couple of days. Just don't stay too long—that's all I ask." I didn't think of Maria. I couldn't bear to.

He got a pen from the Mason jar on the table and signed his name in big black letters at the bottom of the card.

Then he held the card out in front of him and read it off:

"'PERMIT: This certifies that I, Melody O'Bannon Walker, legally wedded wife of Buck M. Walker, do hereby permit my husband to go where he pleases, when he pleases, and to drink what he pleases.

"'AND FURTHER, I permit him to keep and enjoy the company of any lady or ladies he sees fit, as I know him to be a good judge. I want him to enjoy life in this world as I know he will be a long time dead.'"

He ran his finger under my signature, then under his—"Void unless countersigned"—and then he took out his beat-up wallet and inserted that card carefully behind his driver's license. "I want to keep this for reference," he said, and he smiled at me. "In case you go and change your mind."

"I won't," I said, and in all this time, I haven't.

Looking back on it now from the other side of a lot of change— the baby born healthy and christened Melody (Sundance, they decided, was too New Age), Buddy working pretty steady in Emily's real-estate office, Buck and me ready finally to sell the Wilderness and move to an apartment in town with a room for guests—I think, Was I crazy, or what? Some bug bit me, and I stopped being a more-or-less sensible, more-or-less responsible middle-aged woman with a job and a family and turned into some kind of freak.

Buck says I was looking for my youth. Arthur—he drops by to see me every now and then—says I was trying to wear the pants (and he'd let me, still). Buddy when he brings the baby for me to keep over the weekend just smiles his sly smile when I talk about my dancing. Bridget asked me one time if she could see how I did the Tango, and I showed her.

Up and down the hall from the kitchen to our bedroom, that long smooth step—and I felt it again, the silkiness that's neither lead nor follow, and I knew it was all worth it, just for that.

Our FM station plays Big Band music on Saturday nights, and sometimes when Buck's out someplace and I don't have chores to do, I tune in. It's not coming from the Beautiful Skyline Ballroom in Cincinnati or the Roof Garden in Chicago or any of those other places they used to broadcast from when I was growing up in the Purchase. It's just CDs.

All the same, I get into dance position, pull in my stomach, lengthen my spine, lower my shoulders and hold up my head the way Monty taught me, and when the music starts—Waltz, Cha-Cha, Quick-step—I catch the beat and start to move, round and round between the dinette table and the stove, twirls and dips and turns, and my reflection in the window keeps up with me, step for step, and I know I'm still the best social dancer in Santa Fe. And I always will be.

One more thing: right after Buck and I got back from Vegas, I mailed those two round paper firsts to Monty at the studio with a note thanking him for all the trouble he'd taken, teaching me.

He mailed them right back.

This book was set in the typeface Jenson Pro 12 / 16
with an occasional use of Adobe Wood Type font.
It is printed on acid free paper.

www.ingramcontent.com/pod-product-compliance
Lightning Source LLC
Chambersburg PA
CBHW011342010726
47493CB00009B/2921